MW01593481

GIRL ON THE RUN

Book V
A Roseanna Series Novel

Copyright---2002 by Viti Lee Tackett
Library of Congress
All Rights Reserved

ISBN: 1-931600-30-9

Royal Family Publishing
High Point, NC

Printed in United States of America

Faith Printing Company
Taylors, SC

Songs: *A Little Rock* and *Red River* written and recorded by David Patillo. Used by permission.

Dedication

I dedicate this book to my grandchildren, Jason, Josh, John David, Jordan, Laura Lynn, Brittany, and Collin Mitchel. All of you have been blessed to have the warmth of a loving family, and the security of a good home, and I thank God for that.

But there are other kids out there who have not been so blessed; kids who live everyday with abuse, neglect, pain, hunger and fear. To these kids, I also dedicate this book, with a prayer that someone will be there for you, to touch your lives with love and hope, and to show you, through their love, that you do have a heavenly Father who loves you and is watching over you.

Acknowledgements

Thanks to my granddaughter, Brittany Hines, for being the model for Cassie on the cover of the book. Brit, you did a great job portraying the emotions of a young girl on the run.

Thanks to Garry King for taking time out of his busy schedule to take the picture for the cover of the book; and once again, as always, doing a superb job.

Books in Roseanna Series

Roseanna
Belle's Restless Heart
Beyond The Tempest
Rainbow's End
Girl On The Run
Two Roads   (coming soon)

To Purchase Books:
Call Toll Free: 1-866-240-2501
Email: goviti@hotmail.com

Chapter 1

"Mama, let's go to bed," Cassie pleaded for the third time, knowing full well what would happen if they were still up when daddy got home.

Today was second Wednesday of the month and it was payday where daddy worked, and that meant trouble for mama and her. Daddy seldom made it home with his paycheck. He would stop at a bar on his way from the factory and spend most of the money on booze. He became more violent than usual from the drinking, and even more so if mama asked about the money; and mama always asked.

"You go on up to bed, sweetie," her mother said, giving Cassie a big hug.

"No, Mama, I'll wait for you." Maybe, if she stayed down here she could talk mama into going upstairs before daddy got home, and, then, maybe things would be different this time.

Rebecca Bowman pulled her daughter onto her lap and kissed her lovingly. "I love you, my pretty little girl."

"You're the pretty one, Mama," Cassie said, stroking her mother's long blonde hair. Cassie's mother had been blessed with the best of features; tall and graceful, with a perfect oval-shaped face and a flawless complexion that needed no extra help to make it glow, and big blue eyes that should have sparkled, but was dimmed by the life that fate had dealt her.

"That's the only good thing I ever got from my mother." Rebecca said. "I wanted her love, but all she had to give was her looks. Your grandmother was a beauty queen, winning just about every beauty contest around."

1

"Grandmother?" Cassie asked in surprise. Then she nodded. "The trophy room," she said, remembering. On a rare visit to see her grandmother, she had wandered into a room where trophies were displayed everywhere. Grandmother Cassidy had walked in just as she picked up one of them to look at it. Her grandmother had snatched it from her and slapped her hand sharply, with a harsh warning to never come into this room again.

"Those trophies were all she cared about," Cassie's mother said sadly. "She certainly didn't care about me. I think she somehow blamed me for taking away all her dreams of one day becoming Miss America; and she hated me for it."

"Is that why she was so mean---is that why no one liked her?" Cassie asked, remembering her grandmother's sharp tongue and the angry look that was always on her face. "Is that why grandmother never smiled?" Then, without waiting for an answer, she asked another question. "Grandfather Cassidy was nice, wasn't he?"

A warm glow filled Rebecca's insides. She always felt warm and happy when she thought about her father. She nodded. "I don't remember much about him. He left when I was very young. I never knew why he left, but I always figured my mother was the cause of it. I know he loved me, and would never have left me without a good reason. I remember how he smiled when he'd take me on his knee and tell me stories."

"The one about the wonderful little Baby…" Cassie stopped suddenly, and her heart pounded wildly as she heard daddy's car pull into the yard. "Come on, Mama, let's go to bed right now," she urged, hoping they could get upstairs before he came inside; and maybe, he would pass out on the couch and sleep it off. But just then the front door opened and her father stumbled in, mumbling obscenities. "Please, Mama, don't mention the money," she whispered under her breath. But Mama did.

2

"The money! That's all you care about," Evan Bowman ranted in his drunken state.

Cassie waited for the blows she knew would come. She shut her eyes, but she could visualize the scene: she'd lived through it enough that it was etched indelibly in her mind. She clasped her hands over her ears hoping to shut it out. But nothing could shut out the cursing and raging of daddy's voice as he raised his fists in anger.

The first blow came, followed by mama's scream, and daddy's voice ranting more curses. Then another blow and another.

"He's going to kill her this time," Cassie mumbled in horror, knowing she had to do something. She looked around the room and spied her baseball bat leaning against the wall where she had put it earlier. She picked it up.

"Don't hit her again!" she screamed, moving toward her father with the bat poised to swing.

"You stay out of this, you little brat," her father stormed, and knocked her across the room with his fists. He grabbed his wife and started hitting her again.

Still reeling from the blow, Cassie slowly got up, picked up the bat, and moving stealthily behind her father; she raised her weapon high in the air and hit him on the back of the head with all of her might. His knees buckled and he fell to the floor.

She quickly knelt by her mother's side. "Mama," she cried, holding her gently in her arms and weeping as she looked into her battered and bleeding face. "Get up Mama, we've got to get him out of here before he comes to, or he'll kill both of us," she said, helping her to her feet. Together they dragged him outside and left him lying on the ground. They locked both doors with the chain locks so his key wouldn't work, and secured all the windows. Then, they turned out the lights and went to bed in Cassie's room. They held on to each other when the cursing and threatening, and the loud pounding on the door started,

3

along with demands that they let him in. Finally the noise stopped and they heard the tires squeal as he spun angrily out of the driveway. They would be safe tonight.

Cassie's mother held onto to her tightly and ran her fingers over the bruises on her face where her father had hit her. "He'll never hurt you again, my precious baby. Mama won't ever let him hurt you again."

The next afternoon, a police car whizzed by Cassie as she walked home from school. She gasped in horror when she saw it parked in front of her house. Had daddy come back? Had he killed mama? She started to run into the yard, but stopped in her tracks when she saw two policemen coming out of the house with mama between them. Her heart pounded furiously and she started to run to her mother's side, but stopped again when Miss Nelson walked out on the porch. *The woman that takes kids away from their parents and gives them to other people...* "What's she doing here?" Cassie mumbled, jumping behind a clump of bushes before they had a chance to spot her.

Miss Nelson, a tall, spindly woman with short brown hair, was dressed in a severe brown suit and brown low-heeled shoes. She might have been pretty if not for the hardened features reflected in her thin face and green eyes, and the type of clothes she wore. "You go ahead and take her. I'll wait here for the girl. I have a family that's willing to take her in today," she told the policemen, in a sharp voice, that made her seem even less attractive, and then, she walked back into the house.

Cassie watched in horror as the officers put mama in the backseat of the patrol car and drove away. She caught a glimpse of her mother's face as the car passed a few feet from her hiding place. She couldn't hold back the tears as she saw the look of terror on mama's face, the hopelessness in her eyes.

She wanted to run after them, screaming that there had been a horrible mistake, demanding they let mama go,

4

but she couldn't. She had to get out of here before they found her. If that woman gave her to another family, she'd never find out where they were taking mama, and why.

She looked around to make sure no one was in sight, the she started running through the woods. They would be looking for her soon so she had to stay off the roads. She stuck to the thick foliage of the woods and avoided the clearings as much as possible. The red jacket she was wearing would be easy to spot if someone happened to be looking in that direction.

Only the crunching of dry leaves underneath her feet sounded louder than the pounding of her heart, as she ran through the woods in search of a place where she would be safe, so she could try to find out what happened to mama. Why did they take her away? She remembered her mother's words from last night: "He will never hurt you again...I won't let him." Did she kill daddy? "They surely wouldn't arrest her for that," she mused aloud. But she knew they would. None of the good people in their community cared what happened to mama. They knew that daddy beat her, but they would never come forward to testify; as far as they were concerned, mama was a little 'touched in the head', and wasn't worth their time or efforts. "I'm the only chance she has," Cassie muttered, as her nostrils burned like fire, from breathing the cold air, and her throat, dry as cotton, ached for a drink of water. She gasped for breath and sat down under a big tree to rest a moment.

The flood of tears that she'd been holding back gushed out like a shut up dam that suddenly let go of its waters. It all seemed so hopeless. "I'm just a kid," she sobbed, "how can I help mama?" Then she remembered the story that mama had told her; the one Grandfather Cassidy had told mama when she was a small girl, about a Baby that was born a long time ago; a wonderful Baby, with special powers, and a love so big that He would help anyone who needed Him. Mama had told her if she ever got into trouble, just find the Baby, and He would help her.

"How can I find this Baby when I don't even know where to look?" she pondered aloud. She thought she had found him, a few years back, when she had gone into town with mama and daddy during the Christmas holidays, before things got so bad in their family. Maple Hill was a small community town where everyone knew everyone else, and the streets were safe for kids, so mama allowed her to go walking alone, while they did their shopping. She had walked along the streets and stopped to gaze in wonder at a Nativity scene in the yard of a big church in the center of town. She had never been to church, so she looked with awe at the beautiful angels hovering over a stable. She stepped closer for a better look. She saw a baby lying there, and with all the people and animals kneeling down before him, she just knew this had to be the wonderful Baby that mama told her about. She walked over and touched him to get his attention; he was made of hard plastic! He was not the Baby at all. Remembering now, how disappointed she was that day, she began to wonder if she would ever find the real Baby. "I've got to try; for mama," she said, standing up and starting through the woods again.

Briers and sharp leaves scratched her face and hands as she made her way through the thick foliage, but she hardly noticed the pain. Thoughts of mama were troubling her mind. *Why had they taken her away and where was she? Would she ever find her? Could an eleven-year-old girl do what had to be done?* Tears stung her eyes, as she thought of mama, scared and alone. It wasn't fair. Mama had never hurt anyone, so why was this happening to her.

"Will they bring the dogs out to search for me?" she mumbled, as a chill went through her, not so much from the cold, as from the thought of being hunted down by dogs. It was hard to throw a dog off the scent once they were on the

6

trail of something or *someone.* "I don't stand a chance if they get the dogs."

The sun was going down and casting dark shadows in the woods. The cold breeze went right through the light jacket that Cassie was wearing. She shivered as the cold January wind whipped around her, and she wished that she had worn her heavy jacket to school this morning. Darkness would soon fall and she could no longer find her way through the woods. "I'll go as far as I can," she purposed, and started running again. Was she going in the right direction, or was she going around in circles? What if she came out of the woods close to where she went in? She couldn't allow herself to even think that. She had to keep going.

She would have to stop soon and spend the night here alone in the woods. Her heart pounded furiously as panic seized her. She had never spent the night alone before, and certainly not in a place as scary as these woods. She thought about the wild animals that lived here, and roamed the woods at night. She'd heard that they had eyes that could see in the dark. They would be able to spot her before they got close enough for her to see them; and what about when she went to sleep. "I'll have to stay awake," she muttered, trying to calm down. She must not let her fear overwhelm her. She had to keep going. She had to find mama.

"Wonderful little Baby," she said aloud, "if you have the great powers that mama told me about, and if you somehow know what I'm saying, can you please keep me safe tonight, and help me find mama."

Dusk had fallen over the woods and darkness was fast approaching. She could see the lights of a town off in the distance. "That's too many lights for Maple Hill," she muttered, and sighed in relief. At least she was not going to end up in the small community town where she lived.

"I'll have to stop for the night," she muttered again, and realizing how cold it would get before morning, she

7

looked around for a way to keep from freezing. She raked the dry leaves that were scattered over the ground together in a thick pile, the length of her body. She lay down on the pile of leaves and used her backpack for a pillow. She slipped her jacket on backwards so it would be like a blanket. She covered her face with the hood.

She felt the hunger pangs as they growled in her stomach. Her throat was parched and yearned for water. But she knew there would be no food or water tonight. She fought back the tears that were trying to come. She closed her eyes, and out of sheer exhaustion, she fell asleep.

The wind heard the command, and it blew softly on the leaves, gathering them together and dropping them ever so gently over Cassie to form a blanket of warmth around her. Then the wind settled down and didn't blow at all the rest of the night.

The wild animals that usually roamed the woods at night heard the command, and they lay down and slept through the night.

Jack Frost heard the command and he deposited his frosty package on the other side of the woods, far away from the spot where the young girl lay sleeping.

Cassie slept warm and snug in her blanket of leaves, not knowing that she had found the Baby, and He was watching over her.

Chapter 2

Dawn was barely breaking through when Cassie awoke the next morning. She stretched and yawned, raking the leaves off with her hand. "The wind must have blown them over me," she mused aloud and dismissed it from her mind. She could see the lights of the town in the distance. There were not so many lights now, as last night, but there were still enough to guide her in the right direction. "If I can sneak into town, early, when there's no one around, I'll stand a better chance of not getting caught," she mused again, picking up her backpack and heading in the direction of the lights.

Except for an occasional passer-by out for their morning walk, before beginning their busy workday, the streets were empty when Cassie made her way into town. A dog howled off in the distance and she wondered if he was hungry and cold like her. She ducked into an alley so she would not be noticed. Some well meaning person would be sure to spot her and wonder what a girl her age was doing out here on the streets, alone, so early in the morning.

Icicles hung from the roofs of the buildings as she walked through the alley. They were low enough that she could reach them. She broke off one and put it in her mouth. The water tasted so good, as it ran down her parched throat. She was hungry, but quenching her thirst was the most important thing now. She broke off another one, and another. She would look for food later. She shivered as she sat, leaning against a wall, trying to shield herself from the bitter wind. She would stay here out of sight until more people were on the streets, then maybe she

9

could join in with them, without being noticed, and get lost in the crowd.

She wondered where her mother was, and if she was all right. Why did they take her away and what did they do to her? She racked her brain for a possible explanation, but there was no answer. "How can I find you, Mama? Where do I start looking?" she cried, feeling helpless and alone.

Cassie knew she was just a kid and not smart enough to know the ins and outs of finding her mother. Where would she begin? If a kid started asking a lot of questions, wouldn't grownups get suspicious, wouldn't they check her out?

The sun came up and began to spread its sunshine over the town. The buildings shaded most of the sun's rays and kept them away from the alley, but the little that did shine through warmed her.

Cassie's stomach told her that it was time to look for food but where did she start? She didn't have any money and she couldn't steal; mama would never allow that. She walked over to a garbage bin and looked in. She lifted the garbage, piece by piece, until she came to some scraps that had been thrown away by folks who had way too much to eat. She remembered the scraps she'd left on her plate the last time she ate a meal; what she wouldn't give for them right now. The food in the garbage bin was wet and limp and the smell of it made her gag. "I'm not that hungry," she mumbled, putting her hand over her mouth to keep from throwing up. She hurried down the alley, and sat down, leaning against a building.

She thought of the nice clean kitchen at home and of mama's good cooking. She would probably be sitting down right now to homemade pancakes with lots of butter and syrup. She could almost taste them as hunger pains growled in her stomach.

10

"Will I ever find you, Mama?" she cried, as a feeling of hopelessness spread through her entire being; and she wept.

"Pssst." Cassie heard a hissing sound and looked around.

"Over here," a voice called softly.

She looked around again, and saw a boy on the other side of the alley.

"Come here," he called, motioning to her.

She shook her head and looked away.

The boy walked over to her. "You in trouble," he said, more as a statement, than a question.

Cassie didn't look up.

"Listen, kid, if you gonna live on the streets, you gotta wise up; you gotta learn the ropes," the boy told her. "And, you gotta toughen up, too. You can't go round crying or you won't last one day."

Cassie still ignored him.

"You gonna need a friend, kid, and you can't be too choosy out here, so do you want me to help you or not?"

Cassie looked at him, trying to size him up. He was tall and lanky, so she figured he was at least fifteen years old. His dark blonde hair was unkempt and oily. His clothes were grimy and he was dirty. She wondered how long it had been since he'd had a bath or clean clothes to wear. His light blue eyes mirrored sadness and a hardness much older than his years. Everything about his appearance told her to run away, but something in the way he spoke told her to stay. He had offered to help, and since he lived on the streets, maybe she could trust him. "I'll have to trust him," she said to herself. "He's all I've got."

"Well?" he asked, a little put out by her hesitation.

"My name is..."

He put his hand over her mouth. "We don't use real names out here," he told her. "That way if the cops lean on us for information about run-away kids, we don't know

11

nothing. My street name is Duke and I'll call you Little Flower, cause you're so young, and as pretty as a rose that's blooming." He took her hand and lifted her to her feet. "You hungry?"

She nodded. "You got money?"

"No, but I got plenty of know-how, and that's all I need out here."

Cassie cringed, thinking of the scraps in the garbage bin. "I can't eat food out of the garbage," she told him.

"Don't worry," he said. "I gave that up a long time ago, when I learned the secret to getting real food. It's called supply and demand."

"Supply and demand?"

"Yeah. See that grocery store over there," he said, pointing to a building at the end of the block. "They've got the supply and we've got the demand."

"But we don't have any money, how can...surely, you're not talking about stealing," she gasped as the truth sunk in.

"We don't call it stealing out here, we call it survival."

"I can't," she protested.

"You're hungry, right?"

"Yeah, but I can't steal."

"You can't eat out of garbage bins and you can't steal," he said. "Just what do you plan on doing?"

"I don't know, but I could never take anything that wasn't mine."

"Well, excuse me, little princess, for suggesting such a thing," he scoffed. "Are you one of those goody-goody church going folks, who thinks everyone in the world has to live by their rules."

"I've never been to church," she told him, "but my mother has rules to teach me what's right and what's wrong."

"Didn't you run away from home to get away from all those rules?"

"No, I ran away because..." She stopped short of blurting out the real reason she was out here on the streets, then, she changed the subject. "Did you say you could get us something to eat?"

"You wait right here and I'll be back in a little while with the food." He came back a few minutes later with a package of donuts, several bars of candy, and a few cans of soft drinks.

Cassie tried not to think how Duke had gotten the food as she stuffed donuts in her mouth. Was it wrong to eat food that you knew was stolen even if you didn't actually steal it yourself? She was too hungry to ponder the right and wrong of it, or to let it keep her from eating. She stuffed another donut in her mouth.

"Slow down or you're gonna be sick," he cautioned her, "and, this stuff might have to last us all day."

"I'm sorry. I forgot my manners," she said politely. "Thank you for the food, Duke. I know you took a chance getting it."

"Don't mention it," he said. "It's all in a days work out here."

Cassie couldn't comprehend stealing as a way of life. Duke was right; she would never make it on her own out here on the streets. Should she go back home and hope for the best? No, that would mean she had given up on finding mama, and she'd never do that, no matter what.

"You're right, Duke," she said, "I do need help. I'm in a lot of trouble and I don't know what to do."

"You can start by telling me why you ended up on the streets."

Cassie hesitated. Could she trust this young man whom she had just met with her secret? She couldn't see that she had a choice, she certainly didn't know where to

13

start trying to find mama; maybe Duke would have some ideas. She told him the whole story.

"So, that's how you got that shiner," he remarked, pointing to her black eye. "Did your old man hit you a lot?"

She nodded. "Can you help me find mama?"

"Maybe," he said. "We'll start by looking in the newspaper to see if anything's in there?"

"How are we going to get a paper?"

"I know where they keep the old papers that don't sell," he told her. "We'll have to wait until tomorrow to check it out."

"What do we do until then?"

"We could make a list of things to do to help find your mother, but we don't have paper and pencil..."

"I've got some right here in my backpack," she exclaimed, pulling them out and handing them to Duke.

"I'll do the thinking and you do the writing," he said, casually, not wanting her to know he wasn't very good at writing or spelling. He had run away from home when he was in the fourth grade; and, even before then, he hadn't tried too hard to learn how to write and spell.

"Okay," she said, ready to write down his suggestions.

"We're limited on what we can do since we don't have any money," he said thoughtfully. "The newspaper will be our only source of information. We can check to see if there's been a killing, in case she killed your old man. If she did, then we'll know she's in jail. They may also have a listing of who's been admitted to the hospital."

"I don't think they took her to a hospital. She wasn't sick or anything---but, we can check it out, just in case," she added quickly, not wanting Duke to think his ideas weren't good ones.

"Write down that we'll keep an eye out for that woman---the one at your house."

"Miss Nelson?"

14

"Yeah. She probably knows what happened," he said. "If we see her round here, we'll follow her and see where she leads us."

"That's a good idea, as long as she don't see me," Cassie said, beginning to feel better about finding her mother, and also about Duke.

"Now what?" Cassie asked, putting the paper and pencil into her backpack.

"We gotta find a place for you to sleep," he told her.

"How do we do that?" she asked. "I don't have money for a room."

"I can see I got a lot to teach you," he said. "We don't rent rooms out here; we find places to stay for free.

"These free places, are they in a shelter or something like that?"

He shook his head. "The people in those places freak out when they see a kid come in alone, and they want to protect them, so we end up in foster care or worse," he explained. "We have to take care of ourselves."

"How?" she asked, feeling certain that she wasn't going to like the answer.

"Come, I'll show you," he said, and started walking down the alley.

"Is this where I sleep?" Cassie asked, when they stopped in back of a big store.

"No, we just get your bed here," he replied. "This is a furniture store."

Cassie gasped. "Surely you're not going to take something from this store. You'd get caught for sure."

He shook his head again. "You don't know anything, do you," he said, and not bothering to explain, he started walking back down the alley. "We'll have to come back later, after their shipment comes in."

Cassie didn't ask any more questions feeling sure she didn't want to hear the answers. She shivered as she followed him down the alley.

15

"We're gonna have to do something about that," he said, noticing that she was shivering. "We've gotta get you a warmer coat, and I think I know where to find one."

"No, Duke," she said. "I'm okay, really I am." She didn't want to chance him getting caught stealing a coat for her. Part of her reasoning was selfish, she didn't want to be out here on the streets alone; but the other part was because she didn't want him to get into trouble.

"Don't worry, Little Flower, I'm not gonna get caught," he said, as if reading her mind. "We're getting the coat at the Goodwill place and they don't have time to watch everybody, especially during the noon hour when they only have one worker there, so that's when we'll go."

"We?"

"Yeah, I gotta start training you," he said, matter-of-factly, as if he were doing her a favor by teaching her how to steal. "This will be a piece of cake, so it will be a good time to give you some lessons in the art of getting what you need without getting caught."

"Wouldn't they just give us the coat if we asked?"

"Yeah, they probably would, cause they're a bunch of do-gooders, but, what if they started asking questions? Would you want to deal with that?"

She shook her head, sadly, knowing he was right. She couldn't afford to have people asking questions.

Cassie's heart was pounding a mile a minute when they walked into the Goodwill store. Could she do this? Could she steal, knowing it was wrong to do so?

What would mama think? But, if she didn't get a warmer coat, she couldn't stay out here and look for mama. She had to at least try. Following Duke's instructions, she walked over and started trying on coats. She found a blue jacket that fit her, and, following more instructions, she nodded in his direction. He nodded back. That was the signal for her to watch him closely, and when he distracted the clerk, she was to walk outside, wearing the coat, and

16

keep on walking until she reached the alley. She was not to look back or wait on him. She watched until he got the woman's attention, and then she walked out of the store without anyone noticing her.

She hurried into the alley, her heart pounding. She knew she was safe now, but she still felt sick at her stomach. It had all been too easy; she had stolen the jacket without any problems at all. Maybe, that's what scared her the most; taking something that doesn't belong to you shouldn't have been that easy. She felt guilt eating away at her insides. It was as if mama was watching, and had seen everything. Cassie knew she had let mama down; and she cried.

She paced up and down the alley waiting for Duke. "It's been too long," she mumbled to herself. "He should have been here by now." Had they caught him? Should she take the jacket back and confess that she was the one who stole it, not Duke. Didn't she owe him that? Would they put him in jail? "I've got to help him," she mumbled again, and started back to the store.

"Hey, Little Flower, where you going?"

"Duke!" she exclaimed joyously. "They didn't catch you!"

"Of course they didn't catch me," he said, laying an armload of things on the ground. "I went by my place and got this stuff. I'm gonna find a new place to sleep; one nearby, cause you can't stay where I'm stayin', and it's not safe for a girl to be alone at night, out here on the streets."

"Where are we staying?" she asked, remembering the furniture store and wondering if they were going to try to sneak in there and spend the night.

"Come, I'll show you," he said, picking up his stuff and heading down the alley. She grabbed her backpack and followed. He stopped in the back of the furniture store where they'd been earlier. "Okay, pick out your bed," he told her, pointing to several large boxes that had been

17

discarded. "Let's grab a couple of the biggest ones and get out of here before they spot us."

"Are we gonna sleep in those?" Cassie asked, her heart sinking within her.

"Yeah, now get a move on."

They chose boxes that refrigerators had been shipped in and dragged them down the alley.

Finally, Duke stopped. "This will be a good spot," he said. "There's enough light for us to see, but not so much that folks will notice us. He turned the boxes lengthwise, with the open part facing the wall of the building where they were going to sleep that night. "With the boxes turned this way, we'll be protected from the wind in all directions. You should stay warm enough with this around you." He handed her a blanket.

"Thanks, Duke," she said, remembering how scared she was last night when she spent the night alone in the woods. She was glad he would be sleeping nearby.

"We'll finish off the food from this morning and then we need to bed down for the night," he told her. "It gets really cold out here when darkness falls."

She took the food from her backpack and they sat against the wall and ate the rest of the donuts and candy bars, and finished off the soft drinks.

"I'll try to get some fruit tomorrow," he said. "We need something besides all this junk food."

"It tastes good to me," she said, then added thoughtfully, "Duke, I wish there was some way that I could earn at least enough money to buy food for us, so you wouldn't have to steal."

"Yeah, and just what can a kid your age do to make money?" he asked, with a note of sarcasm in his voice, trying to sound tough; but it got to him that she would care what happened to him. It had been a long time since anyone cared about him at all.

"I know how to do housework," she said, "and I can cook a little, too."

"Well, if I run across anyone who needs someone to do housework or a little cooking, I'll put in a good word for you, but, don't hold your breath," he said teasingly, not wanting to upset her, but knowing that's not the way it would be. She'd have to wise up quick; she'd have to steal if she was to make it out here on the streets. The only other choice for a young girl was too horrible to think about, and he'd make sure she never had to do that. He'd tell her the raw facts about life on the streets, but not tonight. Tomorrow would be soon enough. "Now, let's get to bed before it gets too cold out here," he told her.

Cassie spread the blanket inside the box and laid her backpack on top of it. She covered the backpack with her red jacket and used it for a pillow. She lay down and wrapped the blanket around her. She put the blue jacket over her for added warmth. As she lay there in the darkness, thoughts of mama filled her mind. What would they find tomorrow in the newspaper? Had mama killed daddy? Was she in jail? If so, what could they do about it? Where would they go for help? Cassie mulled these questions around and around in her head. Then, as drowsiness overtook her, and her eyelids grew heavy, she sleepily pondered over the events of the past several hours. She had spent her first day on the streets, and thanks to Duke, she had survived.

Chapter 3

Cassie screamed as her world came crashing down on top of her. She saw the shadowy figure of a man an instant before he grabbed her and pulled her to her feet. She smelled liquor reeking from him.

"Hey, you're a girl," he mumbled, squinting to see her in the dim light. "And, a pretty one too. Pretty little girls like you shouldn't be out here alone; I'm taking you with me." He started dragging her down the street.

"Duke!" she screamed. "Help me Duke!"

With the fury of a tornado when it swirls into its target, Duke jumped in front of the man. "Get your hands off her," he demanded, wielding an iron pipe in his hands, ready to strike.

"You stay out of this kid," the man stuttered drunkenly. "I found her, she's mine. You find your own girl."

"Turn her loose right now, or I'm gonna splatter your brains all over this alley," Duke threatened, swinging the pipe at the man's head.

The man let go of his grip on Cassie and started running down the alley, Duke right behind him, swinging the pipe and shouting threats and obscenities that Cassie had never heard, not even from her father's lips.

"Cuse my bad talking," Duke said, after chasing the man a fair distance down the alley. "But I had to put enough fear in him so that he won't come back and try that again."

Cassie burst into tears. "I was so scared, Duke, what if you hadn't been here?" She trembled, thinking of what would have happened if she'd been alone.

He put his arms around her. "I was here, and I always will be," he said, tenderly. "I'll always watch out for you, Little Flower."

"But why, Duke," she asked, with tears streaming down her face. "That man could have had a gun or a knife; why did you risk your life to save me when you hardly know me."

Duke got a far-away look on his face—a sad look. "I have a little sister somewhere. She's about your age." His speech faltered as if he was thinking of words to say. "Her name is Kristina; everyone called her Krissy except me. I called her Honey, cause she was so sweet. I miss my sister and I wonder every day where she is, and if she's okay."

"What happened?" Cassie gasped. "Did she get kidnapped?"

He shook his head sadly. "No, it was nothing like that," he said, as if reliving the whole thing in his mind. "I loved my sister more than anyone else on this earth, but when I was nine years old, my mother took off without an explanation or goodbye; she took Honey with her, but left me behind. I guess she just didn't love me enough to take me too."

"I'm sorry Duke," Cassie said, wishing she could take some of the sadness out of his heart.

"We'd better get back to bed," he said, changing the subject.

"But, my box is ruined," she reminded him.

"Get your blanket and we'll both stay in my box tonight."

They settled down for the night, but neither one could sleep. Cassie looked at Duke. "Is that why you ran away from home?" she asked with concern in her voice.

"Partly, I guess, but it wasn't the main reason," he answered. "It was just Pop and me for awhile, but he was an okay guy, so we made it, until Uncle Cal came to live with us."

"Uncle Cal?"

"Yeah, he was Pop's younger brother, and my father had practically raised him. Pop idealized him and was always there to pick him up when he failed, which was most of the time. Pop couldn't see him for what he really was."

"What happened?"

"As soon as he moved in, my uncle started doing things to me…"

"What kind of things?"

"Uncle Cal started coming into my room at night and doing things to me, things I didn't want him to do." Duke hesitated, not sure if he should be telling her this. "How much do you know about the birds and the bees?" he asked bluntly.

"Mama talked to me about it, and I've heard some stuff," she said. Then the truth sunk in. "He did that to you!" she exclaimed. "I thought men liked women…" her voice trailed off, embarrassed that she had blurted that out.

"Most of them do, but there are a few perverts like Uncle Cal, who likes young boys and preys on them, knowing they can't defend themselves."

"What did your father do when you told him?"

"Pop didn't believe me, and he gave me the worst beating I'd ever had, and told me to never again spread lies like that about my uncle. So I ran away that night and I've been living on the streets ever since."

"How did you make it on the streets as young as you were?"

"The first town I landed in, I met this man named Gus; he took care of me and taught me how to survive on the streets; without him I'd never have made it. I owe

everything to Gus. He was my best friend in the world…"
Tears misted his eyes, as memories of Gus filled his mind.

"What happened to Gus?"

"That's enough talking for tonight," Duke told her. "It's time to sleep now."

But Duke couldn't sleep. Memories of Gus whirled around in his head---haunting memories; memories of the only man who had ever loved him enough to die for him. "Gus," he whispered into the darkness. "Gus, I'm sorry." His thoughts took him back to that night over five years ago; the night Gus died.

"You sick, boy?" Gus asked, feeling of Duke's forehead. Then a worried look crossed his face. "You've got fever. You don't need to be out here in this weather, but it's too late to go to a shelter."

"I'll be all right, Gus," Duke told him. "I'm not feeling that bad, honest." He was feeling really sick, but he didn't want to worry Gus.

"Nonsense," Gus said, looking around for some way to keep Duke dry and warm through the night. "I remember seeing something this morning that will help," he remarked, walking over to a nearby garbage bin. He dug around in the garbage, and pulled out an old tarp. He raked away the snow and ice from the spot where Duke would be sleeping, then he laid the tarp on the ground. The tarp had been about halfway down in the bin, so it was dry. "This weather is not fit for man nor beast to be out in," Gus said, wrapping the blanket around Duke. "I'll get you some medicine in the morning, but you try to sleep now."

Ice and snow covered the streets. The cold north wind blew furiously. No one could survive out here tonight without proper clothing or covering.

The fever raged inside Duke, but he finally slept. He woke once during the night and called out for Gus. When there was no answer he tried to get up to go look for him, but

23

he was too weak and fell back onto his bed and drifted off to a fitful sleep.

Duke felt stronger when he awoke the next morning. He reached down to take the covers off his bed, then, cried out in horror. "No, Gus, no," he gasped when he saw Gus's blanket and coat lying on top of him. He jumped up, stumbling down the alley, looking for his friend. "Why Gus, why did you do it," he wailed, looking all around for him. Then, he spied him, sitting against the wall of a building close by. He ran over to him. His hands trembled as he reached out and touched his face. Then he screamed. Gus was dead. He had frozen to death during the night. Duke fell on his frozen body. "Why Gus—why," he whimpered, tears running down his face. "Gus, please come back. I don't want you to be dead. I love you, Gus, please don't be dead." He cradled his friend in his arms and wept. "I've got to tell someone, I can't let him stay here, like this." He ran down the alley, into the street. A policeman was going into a café. He ran over and tugged at the officer's arm. "Help me, please," he pleaded. "My friend is in the alley. I think he's dead."

The officer looked at him with kindness in his eyes. "You wait right here, son. I'll go check on your friend, and then I'll come back and find you a nice warm place to stay. You won't have to live on the streets any longer." He ran into the alley.

Duke's heart pounded inside him. A policeman meant trouble for him, especially one who wanted to protect him. They would run a check on him and find out who he was; then, they'd send him back home to his father—to Uncle Cal. "I can't stay here," he muttered. But how could he just walk away and leave Gus like that? Gus was his friend—the best friend he'd ever had——but if he stayed... He heard the whistle of a train off in the distance, and he knew he had to be on that train. "I'm sorry, Gus," he cried, and started running toward the train station.

Duke lay there, staring into the darkness, tears rolling down his face. The scenes of that night played over and over in his head. "Gus, I'm so sorry. I didn't want to leave you, but I was so scared. Please forgive me, Gus, forgive me," he cried, as tears soaked his blanket. But he knew there would be no forgiveness; he could never forgive himself; Gus was dead, and dead men can't forgive.

Chapter 4

"Wake up, sleepyhead," Duke said, gently shaking Cassie. "This is the day we start trying to find your mother."

Cassie jumped to her feet. "What do we do first," she asked excitedly.

"First, we find a safe place to stay," he said. "After last night we can't take a chance sleeping out here on the streets."

He saw the disappointment in her eyes.

"Okay," he said, "we'll go by the newspaper office first, then we'll find a place to stay."

They dragged the boxes to a nearby trash bin and walked toward the newspaper office.

"Just walk normal," Duke told her as they walked around to the back of the office where the old papers were stacked in boxes on a big long porch. He casually reached out, took a paper from one of the boxes, and kept walking as if nothing had happened.

Cassie's heart was pounding furiously; and it didn't slow down until they rounded the corner, and no one was chasing them or yelling for them to stop.

"See how easy that was," he said.

She nodded, thinking, again, that it shouldn't be that easy to steal.

They walked to a different part of town. "You wait here while I get our food for today," he said. "If I go to the same store too often, people working there would get to know my face, and become suspicious."

Cassie waited, hating this whole thing about stealing, but she was hungry and this was the only way to get food.

Duke came out. "Come on, we'll find a safe place, now, and I know just where to look. They walked on until they came to a street lined with warehouses.

The stench was overwhelming. Half-starved, angry dogs were fighting over the food in the garbage bins, strewing it all over the street. Cassie held her nose to keep from gagging.

"You'll get used to the smell," Duke assured her, "and the dogs won't hurt you, they're just trying to survive, same as us." He looked in the windows of the warehouses until he found one that was deserted.

"Welcome to our new home," he said, jimmying the door, and walking in. There were empty boxes piled everywhere.

The warehouse was dark and smelled rank and musty. Cassie screamed when her face brushed against a giant spider web.

"Are you hurt?" Duke asked, not being able to see what had happened.

"No, just scared out of my wits," she answered. "Are you sure it's safe in here?"

"A lot safer than out on the streets," he told her, his eyes adjusting to the dim light. "See, it's only a spider web."

"*Only* a spider web," she retorted. "There's probably lots of other little creepy, crawly things in here." She grabbed Duke's arm and stayed close to him.

He walked through the warehouse until he came to a spot close to a window. "This is where we will stay," he said. "This window will give us some light during the day and also let us see anyone that might be passing by."

They cleaned off a space big enough for the two of them, and laid their stuff down. They piled boxes in front of their new 'home' so it would be hidden in case someone came snooping around.

"Now, let's find a place to check out this newspaper," Duke said, leading the way out of the warehouse and down the street. They walked to a nearby park and sat down on a bench. He took a couple of apples out of his coat pocket and handed one to Cassie.

Cassie bit into the apple. She savored its sweetness. "This is so good," she exclaimed. "Thanks, Duke."

He nodded and opened the paper. They scanned the headlines. "There's nothing on the front page about anyone getting murdered; it's all about the war, and terrorism, and stuff like that," he remarked. He handed half the paper to Cassie.

They carefully scanned each page, going over and over each section, making sure they didn't miss anything.

"It looks like your mother didn't kill your old man, after all; so we know she's probably not in jail."

Cassie had mixed emotions. Since mama didn't kill daddy, she wouldn't be in as much trouble, but they still didn't have a clue as to what had happened to her.

"What can we do now?" she asked, tears misting her eyes, beginning to doubt whether she would ever find mama.

"We'll look in the paper again tomorrow," he told her. "And, we still have that woman, that Miss Nelson, we'll keep an eye out for her."

They walked back to the warehouse. Sunlight was shining through the windows and giving more light in the building, and since she could see where she was going, Cassie went snooping around.

"Duke, come look what I found," she called excitedly. "See, it's a mattress," she said when he walked over. "Now, we won't have to sleep on the hard floor."

"We gotta check it first for bugs," he said.

"Bugs?" she asked, shuddering in disgust. "Is there enough light in here to make sure there are no bugs?"

"This will help," he replied, turning on the flashlight he was holding in his hand. "I got this for emergencies, and I'd say this is one."

They checked every inch of the mattress several times; it was dirty, but there were no bugs; and they could live with regular dirt. They dragged it over to the space they had cleaned out and laid their blankets on top of it.

"I need some fresh air," he said. "Let's go for a walk."

They walked down the alley, breathing in the fresh crisp air.

"Stay close to me and let me do the talking," Duke said, as they spied a group of older boys coming toward them. "That's one of the local gangs and we don't want any trouble with them."

Cassie shuddered. She'd heard about street gangs and what they do to people they don't like. She hid behind Duke, as the gang, dressed in leather jackets and wearing big chains around their necks, approached them.

"Hey, dude, who's the kid?" a tall, well built boy, obviously the leader of the gang asked, looking Cassie over. "She your woman?"

Duke shook his head. "She's new on the streets and I'm teaching her the ropes, that's all," Duke replied casually.

"She looking to turn tricks," the boy asked again, grinning and winking at Cassie.

"No, she doesn't want to do that unless it becomes absolutely necessary," Duke answered, a bit nervously this time. "But, if she does decide to do it, we'll let you know."

"You be sure and do that," the gang leader said, more as a threat than a request. "I can hook her up to all the right connections." He motioned to the others and they walked on down the alley.

As soon as the gang rounded the corner, and out of sight, Cassie collapsed into Dukes arms, crying hysterically.

He held on to her tightly. "It's okay, Little Flower, they're gone now."

"What if they come back," she cried, remembering the way the boy had looked at her.

"We'll steer clear of them, I promise."

"Why did that horrible guy ask if I wanted to do tricks; I don't know how to do magic," she sobbed.

Duke thought a moment, trying to figure out a way to tell her. "Out here on the streets, turning tricks has nothing to do with magic," he explained. "A girl gets dressed up like a floozy, stands on a street corner and tries to get a man's attention. When she does, he pays her money; in other words she sells her body to him, and he can do whatever he wants to do to her."

"Have sex!" she cried. "You told him maybe later…"

"I had to say that to get rid of him," Duke said, "but, don't worry, Little Flower, I'd never let that happen to you."

He held her until she calmed down, and then they walked back to the warehouse. They ate the rest of the fruit from this morning and drank water that they had gotten from the park.

"Do we ever get to take a bath or brush our teeth," she asked, the dirt and grime getting to her.

The baths will have to wait 'til summer when we can go swimming in one of the lakes around here, but I will get a toothbrush for you tomorrow, and I have some toothpaste."

"No, Duke, please don't take extra chances for me," she said. "I don't want you to get caught. I can go without brushing my teeth. Please, promise me that you won't do this."

"Don't worry, I can take care of myself," Duke said, trying to act tough, but, again, it got to him that she would care what happened to him. "Now, we'd better get to bed while we still have light enough to see."

They lay down on the mattress and wrapped up in their blankets. "It feels good not to be sleeping on the cold damp ground," Cassie sighed. "Thanks, Duke for finding this place."

"You found the mattress," he reminded her, and, then they both fell quiet, each lost in their own thoughts.

Cassie's mind went back to that terrible gang. What if they found this place where she and Duke were living--- what if they forced her to turn tricks? Duke had promised to protect her---but he was only one person---and there were a lot of them.

Fear gripped her as she remembered the way the gang leader looked at her. She reached over and put her arm around Duke. He took hold of her hand and squeezed it, letting her know that he understood, and, that he would always be there for her; and with Duke close by, she felt safe.

31

Chapter 5

Cassie had been on the streets almost a month now, and they were no closer to finding her mother. They had scanned the paper every day for a couple of weeks, but had come up empty handed. She had almost given up all hope.

They had come across town today to get food. Cassie waited in the alley as Duke headed to a store down the street. She watched as he started into the store, then, drew back in horror as a woman stopped him. It was Miss Nelson! She peeked around the corner just in time to see the woman hand Duke some money. She ran, stumbling, to the warehouse and fell down on the mattress, fear surging through her. How long 'til they found her? What would they do to her? Why did Miss Nelson give Duke money? It all seemed so hopeless, and she let go of the flood of doubts and fears that she had held inside all this time; she felt like she would never find mama; and tears ran down her face.

Later, when she composed herself, she realized that Duke was late getting back. Was he looking for her or had they caught him? Had they taken him away? She felt panic seize her; she couldn't make it out here without Duke. She bolted out of the warehouse, and ran right into him.

"Duke," she cried, "that woman---that was Miss Nelson, the woman that's after me."

"I know; she told me. She showed me your picture, and said she was looking for you; that you were a run-away, and she was trying to find you and take you home."

"That's a lie!"

"I know," he said. "I followed her, hoping to find out something about your mother."

"And did you?" Cassie asked, anxiously.

"No, she went into a couple of official looking buildings, and then got in her car and drove away," he said. "She called you Cassidy."

"Yeah, that's my name, Cassie for short," she said. "Why did she give you money?"

"She asked me to be on the look out, and contact her if I saw you; she gave me her card. I wanted to see what she was up to so I didn't have time to get any food."

"With that money she gave you, we can buy food," she said, grateful that he wouldn't have to steal today.

"Yeah, we'll walk right into McDonalds and order the biggest hamburgers, fries, and milkshakes they have," he told her. "We'll do it tonight to celebrate your job."

"Job?"

"Yeah," he said, grinning proudly, because he had managed to do something he never thought would happen, find a job for her. "A man stopped me on my way back here to the warehouse and asked me if I knew a kid who would like to make fifty bucks, for a couple of hours work, helping his cleaning crew clean a house for a party tonight. And, I told him about you. Do you want the job?"

"Fifty bucks," she exclaimed. "You bet I do!"

Cassie was waiting on the corner where the man said wait. He was supposed to pick her up, in the cleaning truck, at three, and she had gotten there a few minutes early. Duke had come along to make sure everything was on the up and up. He stayed out of sight so he could observe what went on, but where the man couldn't see him.

A cleaning truck pulled over to the curb, and a man opened the door. Cassie looked over at Duke; he nodded; it was the same truck that the man was driving earlier.

Cassie got into the truck and the man drove off.

Duke had a sick feeling in the pit of his stomach as the truck pulled out of sight. Had he done the right thing? Was that man legit?

The man looked at Cassie. "How old are you?" he asked.

"Twelve," she answered, cause eleven sounded so babyish.

"Are you sure you can do this?"

"Yes, I can do it," she said. "I'll work really hard and do everything you tell me."

"Okay, you do that and everything will work out fine," he told her. He drove for several miles before turning into the driveway of a big house, secluded in a clump of tall trees.

"These people must be rich, living in a house like that," she said, noticing that there were no other houses around.

The man opened the door. "You go on, I've got to pick up some supplies," he told her. "Just ring the doorbell and someone will let you in and tell you what to do."

Cassie rang the doorbell and a man opened the door. A stout man whose stomach hung down over his belt. She didn't like the way he was looking at her.

"You sure are a pretty little thing," he said, eying her from head to toe. "I think this is going to work out just fine."

She looked around. There was no one else there. An uneasy feeling tingled down her spine. "The cleaning man had to go for supplies, he'll be back shortly with the rest of the crew, but, I'll go ahead and get started. What do you want me to do first?" She didn't trust the man and felt the need to let him know that the others would be here shortly.

"That man is not coming back, and there is no cleaning job. He just told you that to get you here," the man said.

"I've changed my mind," Cassie told him. "I don't want to stay here." She started for the door.

He grabbed her. "That's not the way it works, little girl," he told her. "I bought you from those people. I laid

34

out big bucks for you. You belong to me, now, and you will do what I say."

"No, I won't!" she said, kicking him on the shin.

"You're a little fighter, I like that," he said, touching her face. "But, we don't have time for that right now. We've got to get the show on the road. I've got big plans for you. Did you ever dream of being in pictures? Well, I'm going to make your dreams come true. Your pictures are going into homes all across this nation and even abroad. You are going to be my little Internet beauty as well as other things---you're here to keep me happy, and I'm not going to waste any more time. There's the bathroom. Go take a shower," he said, shoving her in the direction of the bathroom. "I'll have your clothes laid out here for you. I'll give you five minutes then I want you back out here."

Cassie saw a ray of hope. She'd lock the bathroom door and crawl out the window. She had five minutes to get away from him. Her ray of hope faded when she walked into the bathroom; there was no window, no lock on the door.

As panic welled up inside her, she heard some of Duke's words ringing in her ears. "If you ever get in trouble and I'm not there to help you, keep your wits, don't panic. Look around for a weapon."

Keep your wits. The man had to think she was in the shower, so she took her jacket, shoes and socks off and laid them in a pile on the floor, hoping he wouldn't notice that her other clothes were not there.

Look for a weapon. There was nothing big or heavy enough to knock him out or even stun him enough for her to get away. Then, she saw it---the showerhead. It was a flexible one with a long line.

"I don't hear water running," the man called out. "Now, get a move on. I'm not a patient man."

Cassie hurriedly put her plan into action. She turned the hot water on full blast, but not the showerhead. She turned the nozzle to spray, and held her finger on the button, ready to turn it on. She hid behind the shower curtain, trembling as she waited. She'd only have one chance---what if she missed.

"Your time's up, little girl," the man yelled. "Come on out and let me get a look at you." He paused. "If you won't come out, I'm come in and join you."

Cassie cringed as the door opened and he walked in. She had to wait until he came closer, until he wasn't blocking the doorway.

"Come to daddy," he said, as he reached for the shower curtain.

She stepped out, aimed the showerhead at his face, and pushed the button.

He screamed as the hot water hit his face and eyes.

Cassie bolted out the door.

"You're going to pay for this," he yelled, cursing and holding on to his scalded face.

Cassie ran out the front door, across the lawn, and out into the street. She ran with all her might, trying to get as far away as possible. She knew he would come after her as soon as he could see again; and he'd be in the car. She couldn't out run him, so she had to find a place to hide. Her hair and clothes had gotten wet from standing so close to the shower. Without her shoes and jacket, she would freeze to death in the sub-zero temps tonight. But, she'd rather freeze then for that man to get his hands on her again. Duke had told her how Gus died. She wondered how it felt to freeze to death---how long it took. She looked around, but everything was desolate, no houses, no people, no hiding place. There would be no help for her.

She heard the motor of a car, coming fast, and she knew it was him. She turned onto an empty lot as she heard the car come to a screeching stop, and ran with all the strength she had left in her, but it was not enough. She felt his hands as he grabbed her.

"I've got you, you little bitch, and you're going to pay for scalding my face." He raised his fist to hit her, but stopped. "No, I'm not going to mess that pretty face up, at least not yet," he said. "I'm going to get my money's worth out of you first; and my revenge."

"Please don't hurt me," she pleaded, "please don't."

"That's it, little girl, beg," he smirked. "I like to hear you beg, but there will be no mercy. I'm going to do things to you that you can't even imagine. Before I'm through with you, you'll wish you were dead; but I'm going to keep you around, and I'm going to make you pay every day for the rest of your life." He started dragging her to toward the car.

"No," she screamed into the wind, knowing that no one was around; no one would hear her. "Wonderful little Baby, please help me," she whispered, as the man dragged her roughly across the ground. She kicked and fought, but she was no match for his strength. She knew it was no use. She was back in his clutches, and she couldn't do anything to help herself.

Just then, she heard the frantic honking of a horn. "Help me," she screamed. "Please, help me!"

"Let go of that child," she heard a man's voice yell out.

The man dragging her let out a curse and loosened his grip on her. "Don't think this is the end of it, little girl," he threatened. "I'll find you, and you'll pay double." He ran to his car, jumped in, and sped away.

Cassie felt hands lifting her to her feet. "Don't hurt me, please don't hurt me," she whimpered, cowering in fright, like a cornered animal.

"I'm not going to hurt you, child," the man said, in gentle tones. "I'm going to help you."

He noticed her wet hair and clothes were frozen, and that she was not wearing a coat or shoes. He took his jacket off and wrapped it around her. "Hurry to my car," he told her. "It's warm in there."

She tried to run away from him. He reached out and grabbed her.

"I don't have time to argue with you," he said, picking her up in his arms and hurrying over to his car. He sat her down on the front seat, locked the door, ran around to the driver's side and got in. He took out his cell phone. "I'll call the police…"

Cassie knocked the phone from his hands.

He could see the terror on her face. "The police can wait," he said. "First, I need to get you to a warm, safe place." He reached over to comfort her.

She backed away and sat there, like a frightened little puppy, afraid that he was going to hurt her.

"She's scared to death of me," he said to himself. What had that man done to her to frighten her this way? He wanted to put his arms around her, and assure her that she was safe now, that no one would ever hurt her again, but, first, he had to make her see that she could trust him.

He looked over at her and smiled in a way that only he could. A smile that lit up his face and twinkled his eyes.

Cassie saw that smile and felt better.

He reached over and touched her hand. "I'm Andy Winslow…"

Chapter 6

Andy drove into the back parking lot of the apartment building where he and Angelina lived. "My wife is almost a doctor; she'll know what to do," he said, picking Cassie up in his arms and hurrying up the stairs. He knocked on the back door of the apartment. "Honey, it's me," he yelled, so she wouldn't be afraid to open the door.

"Andy?" she questioned, seeing him standing there with the young girl in his arms.

"She's half frozen," he exclaimed. "What do we do?"

"Put her down on the bed and then run some warm bath water and put some of my bubble bath in it."

"Bubble bath? How does that help?"

"It doesn't really. It just smells nice and girls like to soak in it," Angelina answered, grinning, knowing he would never understand women.

"Get out of those wet clothes and wrap this around you," she told Cassie, handing her a blanket. She hurried into the kitchen, grabbed a thick kitchen towel and stuck it in the microwave for a few seconds. Then she went back to the bedroom. She examined Cassie's feet carefully. "There's no damage," she said, wrapping the hot towel around her feet and gently massaging them. "We need to warm your feet up before you step into that hot water."

Hot water. Cassie trembled as she thought of the hot water she had sprayed into the face of that awful man. Would he find her?

Angelina saw the fear in her eyes and put her arms around her. "You don't have to be afraid. You're safe now. We'll take good care of you." She didn't know what, but she knew something terrible had happened. She'd ask Andy as soon as the girl was in the tub.

39

"The water's ready," Andy announced, coming out of the bathroom.

Angelina helped Cassie into the tub. Then, she went into the bedroom and came back carrying a pair of pink pajamas, a warm robe, and some bedroom slippers. "These might be a little big on you, but they will have to do for now," she said, and walked back into the living room where Andy was waiting.

He told her all he knew about the young girl. "Did she tell you anything?" he asked, hoping maybe she would trust Angelina more than she trusted him.

"Not a word," Angelina said. "Maybe, after she gets something to eat, she'll feel more like talking. Honey, I think it's been a while since she had a decent meal. Would you please fix some hamburgers and fries, and chocolate milkshakes?"

"You sure, baby? Wouldn't vegetables be better for her?"

"Probably so, but I think she needs the comfort of hamburgers, fries and milkshakes," Angelina said. "They always work for me."

"Okay, you're the doctor," he replied, and walked into the kitchen. Soon, the smell of hamburgers filled the air.

Cassie soaked in the tub. It felt so good to take a bath again after a month on the streets. She scrubbed herself briskly with the thick washcloth until she felt clean all over. Then she squeezed the water out of the cloth, letting it run down over her body. She picked bubbles up in her hands and blew them across the room. She couldn't remember ever enjoying anything more than this bath.

Angelina walked in. "Let me wash your hair," she said, "and, then we'll eat. Andy has fixed something special just for you."

Cassie leaned back in the tub and Angelina washed her hair, then poured clear water over her head to rinse off the shampoo. Then she wrapped it in a towel.

Cassie looked at the plate of food that Andy set before her. *Hamburgers, fries, and milkshakes.* "Duke," she whispered, remembering that's what they had planned to eat tonight at McDonalds.

"Duke?" Andy asked, hoping she would say more, but she didn't.

She took a big bite of the hamburger and stuffed fries into her mouth, and before she had finished swallowing them, she grabbed the milkshake and gulped down a big part of it.

Angelina touched her hand gently. "Slow down, honey, there's plenty more where that came from, and, I don't want you making yourself sick."

Cassie continued eating, but slower. Her thoughts were on Duke. What he must be going through. How he must have felt when she didn't return. He'd blame himself, of course. She had to get out of here. She had to find her way back to the warehouse. She had to let Duke know she was okay---but how? She didn't know where she was. She had no idea how to get back to the warehouse. What if she ran into that man again; could she take that chance? She had to; she had to go back to Duke. These people, this Andy and Angelina, would be watching her; so, she would have to be careful and watch for her chance; maybe it would come after they went to sleep.

Angelina set a bowl of vanilla ice cream and some homemade chocolate chip cookies in front of Cassie after she had eaten her fill of hamburgers and fries.

"Thank you," Cassie said, remembering her manners. "Thank you both."

When they finished eating, Angelina took Cassie into the bedroom. "We'll sit in here and do your hair," she said. Then an idea popped into her head. "Andy," she called out, "we're having a girl party in here; no men allowed, so don't try to sneak in." She hoped he would figure out what she was up to; maybe, if she and the girl were alone like this, she could get her to talk.

"You have beautiful hair," she said, fluffing it out with a brush as she blow-dried the long strands of blonde hair.

"I got hair like mama's," Cassie replied, not having a clue what Angelina was trying to do.

"Do you look like your mother?"

"Everyone says so, but I don't know; mama's so pretty."

"You're pretty too," Angelina said, finishing with her hair. She handed her a mirror. "Look at yourself, don't you see a pretty girl in there?"

Cassie looked in the mirror and smiled. "I do look a lot like mama," she said.

"Do you have your mother's name?"

"No, her name is Rebecca, mine is…." Cassie stopped just short of blurting out her name; telling this lady mama's name was too much; she couldn't let them find out her name.

Angelina noticed her reluctance to say anymore so she changed the subject. "Okay, let's do makeovers on each other," she suggested. "Have you ever had a makeover?"

Cassie shook her head.

"Okay, I'll do your makeover first, than you can do mine." She opened her makeup kit and started working on Cassie's face. First, she put some goop on it. "That's a mudpack," she explained. "It will have to set a few minutes. Here, you put one on me, so it can be setting too."

Cassie spread the weird looking stuff on Angelina's face, laughing at how funny they both looked.

"I'll go to the kitchen and get us a snack."

"You gonna let him see you like that?" Cassie asked.

"He's seen me looking worse," Angelina answered, laughing. "I'll be right back." She walked out of the bedroom and shut the door.

"How's it going," Andy asked, in a low voice so that the girl wouldn't overhear. "Has she told you anything--- what's that stuff on your face?" he asked, getting a good look at her.

"This stuff is a mudpack and it will make me beautiful," she told him, giving him a playful kiss, laughing, when he made a face and backed away from her. "The girl hasn't told me much; just that she looks like her mother and her mother's name is Rebecca. She clammed up when I tried to find out her name. But, we're not finished yet. Before we get through, I believe we'll be chatting like best buddies. I need to get back in there. Would you please fix some popcorn and soft drinks for us," Angelina said. "This may be a long night."

He nodded and took her hand and kissed it. "You're not going to sleep in that stuff are you?" he asked, pleadingly. "I'd like to give my wife a real kiss before I go to sleep tonight."

"I promise, when you see me again, I'll be so gorgeous, you won't recognize me," she said. "Just knock on the door when the popcorn and drinks are ready."

"Okay," he said. "It will only take a few minutes."

"Lets get this stuff off our faces," Angelina said, walking back into the bedroom. "You go first. We'll use the bathroom back here."

By the time they finished, the popcorn and sodas were waiting on them. They paused long enough to eat them, then, Cassie sat down in the chair.

Angelina looked her over. "What look do we want?" she mused. "A look of sophistication? A business woman?" She shook her head. "No, let's go all out. Just for fun I'll make you look like a floozy."

You get dressed up like a floozy... "Duke," she whispered. Tears filled her eyes as she remembered his words.

Angelina saw the tears and gently touched her arm. "This Duke, is he special to you----a friend?"

She nodded, and the tears rolled down her face. "He-a--he took care of me."

"Do you want to tell me about it, sweetie? Sometimes it helps to talk about these things."

Cassie shook her head. "I can't---I just can't."

"Honey, we want to help you, but our hands are tied, if you won't tell us what's wrong. What happened to put you in the clutches of that horrible man?" By this time tears were welling up in Angelina eyes. "You can trust us. We'll make sure he never gets his hands on you again, but, first, you've got to talk to me."

Cassie shook her head again, and burst into tears.

Angelina pulled her into her arms and held on to her. "Oh, sweet little girl, if only you'd trust us and let us help you."

"My name is Cassie. They took mama away and I don't know where she is or what they've done to her," she cried. Then she told Angelina the whole story, beginning with the night that daddy had come home drunk and beat them up; how the police took mama away, how she'd run away and ended up on the streets, about the man who had bought her, and how she got away from him.

Angelina was crying as hard as Cassie. "Oh, you poor baby," she said, as anger rose up inside her. "We will find those people who tried to do that to you, and they will pay. I promise, honey."

"What about Mama?" she cried.

"Cassie, you don't have to search alone any longer," Angelina told her, stroking her hair. "Andy's family has lots of money and I promise we will do everything possible to find your mother and bring her back to you. You've had
44

a hard day, so lie down on the bed and rest while I go talk to my husband; and don't you worry, Andy has a way about him for making things turn out right."

Cassie crawled into bed and Angelina pulled the covers up around her. She kissed her on the forehead and turned out the light. She walked out, shutting the door behind her.

Andy saw the tears and took her in his arms. "What's wrong, honey, did she tell you what happened to her? Is that why you're crying?"

She nodded, and clung to him. "Oh, Andy, her name is Cassie," she cried, and told him the whole story, just as Cassie had told it to her.

A mixture of anger and relief showed on Andy's face. "At least she got away from that man before he could hurt her," he said. "He told her that he had bought her?"

"That's what she said."

"I don't like the sound of this, Angelina," he said. "We've got to find out what's going on here."

"Are you going to call the police?"

He thought a moment. "No, I don't think so," he replied. "Cassie was scared to death when I started to call them; and they did take her mother away. We can't afford to trust any of the local police. I'll call Kent. He'll know what to do."

"Good idea," she said, as he dialed the number.

When Kent answered, Andy explained the situation to him.

"I don't like the sound of that," Kent told him. "Keep a close eye on the little girl. I think she may be in grave danger. Let me call Chief Bristol of the FBI and get his input on this," Kent continued. "I'll call you back as soon as I find out anything."

"Thanks Kent," Andy said and hung up the phone.

"Honey, Kent thinks that Cassie may be in danger and says to keep a close eye on her. I can watch her tomorrow while you're at school, but what about tonight? You think she might try to sneak out of here?"

"She's very worried about Duke, and wants him to know she's okay, so yes, I think if she wakes up during the night, she will try to go to him."

"Well, she can sleep in the bedroom with you and I'll sleep out here on the couch," Andy said. "That way if she tries to sneak out, I'll be here..."

"Sweetheart," Angelina broke in, "a herd of wild horses could stampede through here and you would sleep right through it, so I don't think you're going to hear a young girl sneaking out."

"You're right," he said. "I'll lock both doors with the keys so they can't be opened without them, then I'll put the keys under my pillow."

"That should do it," she said, giving him a goodnight kiss, and another, and another. "This is the first night we have slept apart since we got married. I'm going to miss sleeping in your arms."

"Me, too," he said, giving her another goodnight kiss. He walked with her over to the bedroom door and gave her one final lingering kiss. The he went to bed on the couch.

The ringing of the phone awoke him early the next morning. It was Kent.

"Andy, does anyone know the girl is there with you?"

"No," Andy answered, getting a worried look on his face.

"Keep it that way," Kent said, in a serious tone. "I talked to Chief Bristol last night and he made some phone calls. He thinks this is really big. They suspect that there is a child slavery ring operating in several states and he thinks that's what this is."

"Child slavery ring?" Andy asked, puzzled.

"Yeah, it's where kids are sold to unscrupulous people, usually men, who want to use them for sex and pornography; the sad thing is, that the people who sell them

46

are sometimes the very ones who are supposed to protect them," Kent said, a catch in his voice. "Thank God, the little girl got away, and thank God you came along when you did."

"He is the one to thank," Andy agreed. "I wasn't even supposed to be on that street. I turned onto it by mistake, and only realized that I was on the wrong street seconds before I heard her scream."

"Thank God for putting you in the right place at the right time," Kent said. "Andy, you're going to have to get her out of there, take her somewhere she'll be safe. She is the only lead the FBI has to this slavery ring, and those people are going to be after her. They will leave no stone unturned, and they will find her if she stays in that area."

"But where will she be safe?"

"I was thinking back home on the bayou with Roseanna and her family," Kent told him.

"But wouldn't that put all of them in danger?"

"Who would think to look there?" Kent reasoned. "It's such a small place, and, it's only claim to fame is the fact that Roseanna lives there; and no one would ever link the little girl to Roseanna, so I believe the margin of danger is minimal, if any at all."

"I'll talk it over with Angelina and see what she thinks, but I can't take it on myself to put our family at risk."

"Okay, but you need to get her out of there as quickly as possible, and secretly, if you can. No one must know that you have seen this girl, or you and Angelina could be in danger, too."

"I'll call my dad and see if the company jet is available; if so, we can fly out tonight on it," Andy said. "What about the boy, Duke. Cassie won't leave unless she knows he's okay."

"We've taken care of that," Kent assured him. "Before the weekend is over, Chief Bristol will have an undercover agent there on the streets with him. But, Andy, the chief pointed out that we've got to consider the possibility that the boy could be a part of all of this; that he might have turned Cassie over to them willingly."

"God forbid," Andy said. "Cassie would never get over it if Duke betrayed her."

"Just let her know that he'll be safe, and get her out of there before the trail leads to you."

"Okay," Andy told him, and hung up the phone.

He pondered a moment on what to do. Should he follow Kent's advice and take her home to the bayou. She'd probably be safe there, but what if they found her; what kind of trouble would that bring down on the heads of the people he loved so dearly. "I'll call Brad," he muttered. "He'll know what to do."

Chapter 7

Meanwhile, back home in south Louisiana, Belle's heart was singing; she snuggled close to Jesse, as they drove down the highway, on the way to her mother's house to pick up the kids. She sighed contentedly and laid her head on his shoulder. They had worked things out, and he had come home last night. Life was good again.

"I'm so happy, Jesse," she said. "This is the best day ever. We're back together; Brad is bringing Roseanna and the baby home today, and we're all going to be at Mama's tonight for supper. It's been a long time since you were at the supper table with all of us. I can't wait to spring our wonderful surprise on my family. They're going to be so happy."

Jesse looked forward to being with the family, but nagging doubts filled his mind. He wasn't sure that they would welcome him back. He recalled the tensions between them when he and Belle were having problems, and how her father had jumped on him when he found out about Pamela. He had missed all of them and hoped things turned out well, so they could be the happy family that they were before he messed up Belle's life.

He pulled over into a small roadside park and turned off the engine. "Belle, there's something I want to talk to you about before we go on to your parents house," he said, with a serious look on his face. "My wedding band."

"Oh---that," she replied, remembering the hurt she had felt the day Jesse gave the ring back to her; the day he had moved in with Pamela.

"You didn't get rid of it," he gasped. "I loved that ring."

"You loved it, Jesse?" she remarked, raising her eyebrows. "Then, why did you give it back to me? If it was so important to you, why didn't you keep it?"

"Honey, I didn't give the ring back to you because it wasn't important to me, but because it was. It was a symbol of your love for me, and your trust in me. I had betrayed both your love and trust, and it was hard for me to live with that. The ring was a constant reminder of what I had done, and what I had lost. I knew I wasn't fit to wear it, so I gave it to you, thinking that it was important to you too, and you would keep it forever."

"And, what about those hateful things you said to me?" Belle asked, as memories of that day played through her mind. She wished he hadn't brought up the subject of the ring, causing all those hurtful memories to surface.

"Honey, we talked about some of this yesterday, but I want to explain something to you that I didn't tell you then. I said most of those things to you deliberately. I knew you still loved me in spite of everything. I knew you were hurting, Belle; and I loved you too much to hurt you any more. I knew as long as you loved me, you could never get on with your life, so I said those things to you, hoping that you would hate me, and could put me out of your heart forever; and be happy again. I never meant to cause you more hurt."

"I tried to hate you, Jesse, but, no matter how much you had hurt me, the love I felt for you wouldn't go away."

"And, I'm so thankful it didn't." He pulled her to him and kissed her. "I love you so much Belle," he said, "and I don't blame you for getting rid of the ring. I suppose we can buy another one, but that one was special to me."

"It was special to me too," she said, taking a small box from her purse. "I put this in here, meaning to pawn it, but I could never make myself do it. Here's your wedding band, Jesse. You can put it back on your finger where it belongs."

"No, I want you to do that, Belle, but first I want to do this," he said, slipping her ring off her finger. "Honey, the first time I put this ring on your finger, I made vows and promises to you that I didn't keep; now I want to renew those vows."

He took her hands and looked into her eyes. "Belle, I could never find the words to tell you how very much I love you. You are the best part of me; you're everything that I want to be. You're my hero. I am amazed by the goodness of you. In spite of all the hurtful things I did, you never let your feelings show in front of the kids; you made sure they kept on loving me and respecting me as their father. How can I ever thank you for that?" Tears misted his eyes. "Honey, I'm nothing without you, but with you by my side there are no limits to how far I can go. You are the essence of me, the fulfillment of all my dreams. I am so blessed and proud to have you as my wife, and I promise, Belle, that from this moment forward, for all the days of my life, I will be faithful and true to the promises I make to you today, and also to the ones I made to you on the day you became my wife. The worse day of my life was the day I broke the sacred vows I made to you on our wedding day, and, I will spend the rest of my life making it up to you." Tears were rolling down his face as he slipped the ring on her finger. "I love you, Belle, and I will honor you, and cherish you, and I will never put anyone or anything on earth before you."

Belle took his hand. "I accept those vows you have made to me today, and I regret the things I did that hurt you. In spite of everything that happened, Jesse, you are a man of integrity and honor. I am blessed and proud to be your wife, and I promise that from this day forward, I will always put you first, above all others, and I will love you every day of my life." She slipped the ring on his finger.

He pulled her into his arms and kissed her. "Now I'm really home," he said.

"Hello," Belle yelled, a while later, as they walked, hand in hand, into her parents house.

Ellis LeBlanc turned to greet his daughter. Anger flashed in his eyes when he saw Jesse. "What's he doing here?" he demanded.

"Daddy," Belle exclaimed happily. "Jesse came home last night. We're back together."

"Over my dead body!" he ranted. "Jesse Lawrence, get out of my house and get out right now!"

Jesse turned to leave. Belle grabbed his arm.

"No, Jesse, you're staying," she declared, defiance ringing in her voice.

Roseanna walked in just then and stared in disbelief when she saw Jesse standing there. "What are you doing here?" she stormed. "Haven't you hurt my sister enough? Now, get out of here and leave her alone!"

"Roseanna, you don't understand," Belle explained. "Jesse and I worked things out; we're back together."

"How did that scum weasel his way back into your life?" Roseanna asked, angrily. "I won't allow it, Belle, he's not going to hurt you again." She turned to Jesse. "Now get out of here, Jesse. Go back to that whore you've been living with. You're not fit to live with decent folks..."

"That's enough!" Belle screamed, bursting into tears. "How dare you treat Jesse like that, and, how could you do this to me?"

Jesse put his arm around her. "Belle, honey, I don't want to cause trouble between you and your family."

"You're not the one causing the trouble, Jesse," she said. "I've got a few things to say to my family, and then I want you to take me home."

She looked at Roseanna and her father, tears running down her face, anger flashing in her eyes. "I came here today, happier than I've been in a long time, anxious to share my good news with you, and what do you do? You insult the man that I love; you order him out of this house.

52

Well, I want you to know that we're back together; nobody is ever going to tear us apart again, and that includes the two of you. If Jesse is not welcome in your homes, then I am not welcome, and I won't be back!"

"Belle, wait," Roseanna pleaded tearfully, as her sister stormed out the door, holding on to Jesse's hand.

"Mikey. Annie," Belle called. They came running from the backyard where they were playing.

"Mommy," they yelled; then seeing Jesse standing there, they ran into his arms.

He scooped them up and carried them to the car. They were hugging and kissing him, both at the same time. He strapped Annie in her car seat, while Mikey adjusted his seatbelt securely around him. Jesse got into the front seat. Belle slid under the steering wheel; the tires squealed as she spun out onto the road.

Blanche LeBlanc walked into the living room just as Belle and Jesse ran out the door.

"What's wrong with Belle?" she asked, not knowing that Jesse was with her. "What happened here?"

"She had Jesse with her, and I guess things got out of hand," Ellis LeBlanc said, feebly.

Blanche hurried to the door to try to make things right with Belle and Jesse, but the sound of squealing tires told her she was too late. She walked back into the house.

"Ellis LeBlanc, how dare you drive Belle and Jesse out of our home!" she stormed, anger flashing in her eyes.

"Honey, slow down," Jesse cautioned, as Belle sped down the highway.

She nodded and eased her foot off the gas pedal. "I'm sorry," she said. "I didn't realize how fast I was going."

"I thought we were going to eat with Grandma Blanche," Mikey said.

"We changed our minds, we're going to eat at home," Belle told him.

"How would you guys like pizza for supper?" Jesse asked.

"Yes," they yelled, with happy smiles on their faces.

Suddenly the happy smile on Mikey's face was replaced with a worried frown. "Why are you here, Daddy?" he asked, remembering the times Jesse had come to see them only to leave again.

"Daddy's home to stay, baby," Belle said.

Mikey looked at his father. "You gonna stay for real?"

"Yes, son, I'm going to stay for real."

"And, the divorce?"

"The divorce is off," Jesse assured him. "Mommy and I love each other and we're going to stay together forever."

"In the same house?"

Jesse's heart ached as he realized how much his son's trust in him had been damaged. "Yes, son," he answered with a catch in his voice, "Mommy, Annie, you and I are all going to live in the same house and be a family again, the way we used to be."

Mikey smiled. "Thank you Mommy and Daddy," he said happily. "And, thank you, God, for hearing my prayers."

"Have you been praying that we wouldn't get divorced?" Jesse asked.

Mikey nodded his head. "Uncle Brad and me made a pact that we would pray every day for God to stop the divorce, and He did. He does listen to little boys."

"You bet He does," Jesse said, a lump in his throat. He reached back and squeezed his son's hand. "Thank you, son, for praying for us."

Mikey squeezed his father's hand with all his might. "I'm glad you're home, Daddy. I'm glad God answered our prayers."

"Me too," Jesse said, taking his cell phone from his pocket. "I'm going to order the pizzas so we can pick them up as we go through town." He took out his address book and dialed the number.

Ellis LeBlanc paced the floor, worrying about the trouble he was in with his wife, and also racking his brain, trying to think of a way to get Belle out of Jesse's clutches.

Brad walked in. He had been out all afternoon taking care of church business that had fallen behind because of all the time he had spent at the hospital with Roseanna and the baby. "Hi everyone," he called, walking into the living room.

Roseanna ran into his arms, crying.

The color drained from his face. "Sweetheart," he gasped, "has something happened to the baby?"

"No," she shook her head, "he's fine. It's Belle, she hates me, and it's all Jesse's fault."

"What's he done now?" Brad asked, a twinge of anger in his voice.

"He--conned Belle--into letting him--come home," Roseanna sobbed.

"They're back together," Brad exclaimed. "That's great!" He paused. "What's the problem here? This is what we've been hoping and praying for."

Ellis LeBlanc snorted angrily. "Maybe it's what you've been hoping and praying for, but not us, and we told him so, loud and clear."

"What, exactly, went on here?" Brad asked, frowning, certain that he wasn't going to like the answer.

"I ordered him out of my house," Ellis stated.

"And, I told him to go back to that whore he's been living with and leave my sister alone."

"You didn't," Brad gasped. "What were you thinking? Belle loves Jesse with all her heart, and she could never be happy without him; the kids adore their father and they need him there with them."

"And, what about when he decides to leave them and go back to that tramp," Ellis snapped. "I'm not going to stand around and let him hurt them again."

"We were just trying to protect Belle, and she turned on us, said she was never coming back," Roseanna cried, tears running down her face, as thoughts of never seeing her sister again flashed through her mind. "You don't think she really meant it, do you Brad?"

"I wouldn't blame her if she never spoke to either one of you again," Brad said bluntly. "This is her decision to make; after all it is her life. She came to her family to share her happiness with us, and what do you do, you insult the man she loves; so she had to make a choice between Jesse and you, and she chose Jesse. I hope you're satisfied," he continued, looking angrily at them. "Belle needed your support, not your meddling." He headed for the door.

"Where are you going?" Roseanna asked, shaken by his words.

"I'm going to see Belle and Jesse and try to undo the damage you two have done."

Roseanna burst into tears again. "You're right, Brad. I did a terrible thing and I've got to make it right, so I'm coming with you."

"You can't do that, sweetheart. You just got out of the hospital today and made the trip from town; you can't turn around and do it all over again. I'll apologize for you."

"No, Brad, I've got to say what needs to be said, so I going, and that's final."

Brad looked at Mama. If anyone could talk some sense into Roseanna, she could.

Mama shook her head. "One thing's for sure," she said, "when Roseanna makes up her mind to do something, no one can change it; so I'll make a deal with you. I'll keep the kids on two conditions; you eat supper before you leave, and Roseanna takes it easy on the trip into town."

"Agreed," Roseanna said, hugging her. "Thanks, Mama."

"Oh, by the way," Brad remarked as they walked into the kitchen, "Andy called and they are coming home for the weekend. I invited them to stay with us, if that's okay with you, Roseanna."

"That's fine, honey."

"Are you sure it won't be too much on you, sweetheart?"

"I'm very sure," she said. "Now, let's dig into this food so we can go. I can't rest until I make things right with Belle and Jesse."

Brad kept quiet about the reason for Andy and Angelina's trip home. It would be better if they heard it tomorrow after they met the little girl.

Chapter 8

Belle had just finished cleaning up the kitchen, when the doorbell rang. She wiped her hands on a towel and opened the door. "What are you doing here?" she asked, anger flashing in her eyes.

"I'm here to talk to Jesse…"

"He's busy," Belle snapped, trying to shut the door.

"I'll wait," the visitor said, pushing her way past Belle, into the foyer.

"Jesse has nothing to say to you, so please leave," Belle told the unwelcome guest.

"Well, I've got something to tell Jesse and I'm not leaving until I talk to him." And, with that, Pamela walked into the den.

"He's not interested in anything you have to say," Belle told her angrily. "He's home with his family now…"

"Not for long," Pamela taunted. "When he hears what I have to say, he'll come running back to me."

Belle's heart sank within her. "She's pregnant," she muttered under her breath. "She's here to tell Jesse she's going to have his baby."

"So, do you tell Jesse I'm here or do I start yelling?"

"He's putting the kids to bed," Belle said. "He'll be down as soon as he finishes."

"May I?" Pamela asked, taking off the knee length black fur cape she was wearing, laying it on the back of the couch and sitting down.

"By all means, make yourself right at home," Belle said sarcastically. Her heart sank again as she looked at the beautiful woman sitting before her.

The bright red dress Pamela was wearing fit perfectly, from it's low cut neckline to the short mini skirt, clinging to her in all the right places. "Brazen hussy," Belle muttered to herself. Pamela had to know that red was Jesse's favorite color; and the way she looked in it would surely get his attention. Her blonde hair fell over the shoulders of the dress, in long spiral curls, and brought out the highlights of her perfectly made up face. Her eyes sparkled and her rosy cheeks glowed. Everything about her was perfect. "Even the perfume she's wearing probably cost more than what I spent on my entire wardrobe this year," Belle groused to herself.

She paled in comparison. Still peaked from her bout with the flu, her cheeks lacked the rosy glow they usually had. She looked at the jeans and bulky sweater she was wearing and wished she had dressed more alluringly. She felt drab and ugly sitting here beside Pamela. She scooted her feet under the couch, trying to hide her gawky sneakers. "That witch had to know, that by coming here, she would catch me off guard, and I wouldn't be dressed to kill like she is," she fumed silently.

It was evident; Pamela was here for one reason, and one reason only, to seduce Jesse.

Belle had the urge to strangle her. She couldn't stay in the same room with her so she jumped up. "I'll tell Jesse you're here," she muttered awkwardly and took off up the stairs.

Jesse was coming out of Mikey's room when he spotted Belle. Her face was ashen; tears brimmed her eyes. He shut the bedroom door and hurried over to his wife. "What's wrong, honey?"

"Pamela's here," she sobbed. "Oh, Jesse, I think she's pregnant."

The color drained from his face. "Did she say that?"

"No, but she hinted at it."

"Let's not borrow trouble," he said, pulling her into his arms. "And, honey, no matter why she is here, it will change nothing between us; I'm home to stay. Now, let's go see what she has to say." They walked hand in hand down the stairs.

"Pamela, if you're here to tell me that you're pregnant, I'm not buying it," Jesse said bluntly. "You're too smart to let yourself get pregnant when you don't even like kids."

Pamela walked over and cupped his face in her hands. "You know me so well, Jesse, but why wouldn't you, after all we've been to each other," she said smugly, looking at Belle. "Of course, I'm not pregnant, but I can understand why you would think that, after all the..."

"Get on with whatever it is you want to tell me, then please leave," he snapped, angry that she would try to hurt Belle this way.

"First, Jesse, I'm asking you to move back into our home with me."

"We don't have a home," he corrected her. "This is my home, Belle's and mine. This is where I'm going to stay. Now, get on with it. My wife and I would like to be alone."

She took some documents from her purse. "Take a look at this before you make any hasty decisions," she smirked, handing him the papers. "I don't want you to do something that you'll regret later."

Jesse glanced over the papers. "This is the contract to your house, so what does that have to do with me?"

"Take a good look and you will see that your signature is on the contract."

"I don't remember signing that," he told her.

"Of course you don't remember, darling," she said coyly. "You were too drunk to remember anything that day, so I'll refresh your memory. It was the day of the hearing and we were celebrating you moving in with me."

He put his arm around Belle. "I still don't remember signing those papers."

"Well, you did," she snapped. "See, that's your signature."

Jesse looked and nodded. It was his signature. "Pamela, if you think owning half of that mansion will entice me to come back to you, think again," he said. "Nothing on this earth can ever get me away from the family I love."

"Don't be too sure, Jesse; wait until you hear the rest of it." She looked over at Belle, a smirk on her face.

"That day at the hearing when the judge decreed a six months waiting period, I was afraid that you might pull a stunt like this, so I took steps to protect myself. You made commitments to me Jesse; you promised you'd always be there…"

"There's no way that's going to happen."

"You forget, darling, I'm a very smart lawyer and when I want something, I know how to make it happen. Before I came home that day, I had a special contract drawn up for the mansion, making you and I equal partners."

"I don't want to be partners with you in anything, so I'm giving up my rights to the house," he said. "Where do I sign?"

"Jesse, Jesse," she said, shaking her head. "It's not that simple. You know me well, and you know that I'm smart enough to come up with a binding contract that you can't just sign away."

"What have you done?" he asked, a frown knitting his brow. He did know Pamela. She was a very smart lawyer.

"I had a special clause written into the contract stating that you and I will each pay an equal amount for the house. I also financed it with a balloon note, due and payable in full, six months after the hearing. So my dear, you must come up with a million dollars, in three weeks, or lose everything you own."

"I don't have that kind of money and you know it!"

"No problem," she said. "Move back in with me and I'll pay the entire note, and you can keep your house, your bank account, your car, everything----see, it states right here that if you default on the loan, they get everything you own, including your business, and every penny you make from now on, until the debt is paid in full. So, Jesse, if you stay here with sweet Belle, you lose everything; and all of you will end up on the streets, penniless. Is that what you want for your family? Think it over, Jesse, but don't take too long. I'm not a patient woman."

Belle had been quiet up until now, but she couldn't hold back any longer. She got right in Pamela's face. "We don't have to think it over Pamela. Jesse stays put. Even if we lose everything, we still win, cause we'll have Jesse; and having him is worth more than all the money in the world," she said defiantly. "Now get out of our home before I throw you out!"

"I'll be waiting, Jesse," Pamela remarked sweetly, completely ignoring Belle. She leaned over and kissed him before walking out the door.

Jesse slammed the door behind her, then, pulled Belle into his arms. "I'm so sorry, baby, for bringing this all down on you."

Belle had sounded brave in front of Pamela, but now she fell to pieces. "What are we going to do," she cried. "Please tell me there's a way out of this."

He shook his head. "I don't see a way out, Belle," he said, tears misting his eyes, as he thought of the consequences. "I can't let you and the kids end up on the streets, and there's no way I can come up with that kind of money."

"You can't be thinking about going back to her," Belle gasped, horrified.

"I'd die first," he said. "Belle, the only way out of this, may be, if I walk out of your life forever. We can go ahead with the divorce, I'll give everything to you, that way Pamela can't touch it..."

"No!" she cried. "I'll never agree to that! Jesse, don't you know that all this stuff means nothing to the kids and me unless you're here with us. Sink or swim, we're in this together; wherever you end up Jesse, the kids and I will be there with you." She burst into tears just as the doorbell rang again.

"What does she want now?" Jesse exclaimed angrily, yanking the door open. "You bitch, what are you doing..."

"That's uncalled for, Jesse," Brad said, angrily. "I know Roseanna was rude to you, but that doesn't give you the right to call her names."

"I'm sorry," Jesse stammered. "I didn't mean that for you, Roseanna. I thought Pamela had come back."

"Pamela was here?" Roseanna asked, looking over at Belle, and, seeing her in tears, rushed over and took her sister in her arms.

Belle pulled away. "She came here to break some news to Jesse; news that she thought would bring him running back to her."

"She's pregnant!" Roseanna exclaimed.

"If only it were that simple," Jesse sighed, and told them the whole story. "So, if I don't come up with a million dollars in three weeks, we're out on the streets."

"We'll give you the money," Roseanna said.

"I would never be able to pay you back," Jesse replied.

"You wouldn't have to pay us back," Roseanna told him. "Brad and I have more money than we can ever spend; and, you're family."

"Not any more," Belle lashed out. "You made it clear how you feel about Jesse; and we'll end up on the streets before we come to you for charity."

Brad could see the situation was about to get ugly so he spoke up. "Belle, I'd like some coffee. How about you and me fixing some?" This would give Roseanna a chance to talk to Jesse alone.

Roseanna walked over and touched Jesse's arm. Tears were in her eyes. "Jesse, I'm so sorry for the hateful things I said to you. I don't know what got into me."

"I don't blame you for hating me, Roseanna. I hate myself for what I did to Belle."

"I don't hate you, Jesse. I love you. You're like a brother to me." The tears were rolling down her face now. "When I think of how you jumped into those stormy waters to try and save Brad and Isabelle, risking your life to save theirs; and then how you put your life on hold to be there for me when we thought they had drown...Jesse, I'm so ashamed. Can you ever forgive me?"

He took her in his arms and kissed her on the forehead. "Of course, I'll forgive you, Roseanna; that's what families do. Now, dry your tears and let's forget that it ever happened."

"Thank you," she said, wiping her tears. "I hope this means you will accept the money Brad and I offered you."

"No, I can't do that."

"But, if you've forgiven me..."

"It has nothing to do with that," he assured her. "I can't take money, not even from family, that I know I can never pay back; but thanks for offering."

"Well, we'll just have to come up with another way out of this," Roseanna told him, "cause I promise you, this is one battle that Pamela is not going to win."

Brad and Belle walked in from the kitchen with mugs of hot steaming coffee in their hands.

"Let's put our heads together and figure out a way to get you out of this mess," Roseanna said, as Belle handed her a cup of coffee.

Belle put her arms around her sister. "Thanks for caring and I'm sorry about before."

"I'm sorry too, Belle, about everything. Jesse has forgiven me and I hope you will too."

Belle nodded and kissed Roseanna. "Now, go lie down on the couch. I don't want you getting sick again."

"Well, I am a little tired," she said, "and I guess I can think as well laying down as I can sitting up. I told Jesse that we're not going to let Pamela win. There's got to be a way out of this, and we're going to find it, if it takes all night."

Brad shook his head. "No, sweetheart, I've got to get you home soon. You're in no shape to be up this long; and, I promised your mother. So, as soon as we finish our coffee, we'll be going."

"Okay," she said, reluctantly. "Jesse, is there any thing that the loan company can't touch, money that you can live on in case we don't figure a way out of this before the note comes due?"

He shook his head. "I don't know of any. They'll get everything that's in my name; or Belle's and mine."

Belle spoke up. "Yes, there is some money, some investments that Jesse doesn't know about. I never told the family this, but when Jesse and I were separated, he deposited a large part of his earnings each week into my checking account for the kids and me to live on." Tears were misting her eyes, "I made more than enough working with Lance for us to live on, so Lance invested the money Jesse gave us, and, it's done really well. We'll have enough for a down payment on a house; and we can live on the money I make."

"Are you sure that the loan company can't get that money since you and Jesse were never divorced. Wouldn't it be like community property?"

"I don't think so," Belle said. "The first time I talked to my lawyer, the day after I kicked you out, Jesse, he fixed a legal document stating that I was no longer responsible for Jesse's debts. I'm sorry, honey, but he didn't want to take the risk of me getting stuck owing a lot of money."

"That's great, Belle," he said. "I'm not offended. I'm glad your lawyer thought of protecting you like that, and now we have a really good reason to be glad about it."

"I've got to get Roseanna home," Brad said. "We've got three weeks to come up with a solution and between all of us, we should think of something."

"I want all of you to come to our house for supper tomorrow night," Roseanna said. "Andy and Angelina are coming home for the weekend and they are staying with us; Andy wants to talk to all of us together, so the whole family will be there."

"Won't that be too much on you, sis?" Belle asked with concern.

"No, I won't have to lift a finger. The family gathering was Andy's idea, so he's doing all the cooking and he's a very good cook." Roseanna looked over at Brad, wishing she hadn't mentioned that Andy was a good cook. Would it remind him of the past and all the things that she and Andy had shared?

After Belle and Jesse were in bed, her thoughts went back to Pamela and how beautiful she looked tonight. Did Jesse notice? He'd said all the right words when Pamela was here, but how did he really feel? She had to know, and she had to see Jesse's expression when she asked him, so she turned on the light, raised up on her elbow, looked him in the eye, and asked him straight out.

"Jesse, did you notice how beautiful Pamela looked tonight? Dressed in my sweater and jeans, I must have looked like an ugly duckling, up beside her."

"I love you in sweater and jeans," he said, hoping to put her mind at ease.

"Yeah, but don't tell me you didn't notice how sexy she looked, all diked out in red, and wearing that knock out perfume."

Jesse bit his lips to keep from grinning. "Yeah," he said, dreamily. "When I walked down those stairs and saw her standing there, looking so incredibly sexy, I wanted to throw her down on the couch, rip her clothes off, and make mad, passionate love to her; but you were there so I couldn't."

"Jesse Lawrence, stop teasing me!" she exclaimed. "You'd never do that!"

He laughed and pulled her into his arms. "Of course I'd never do that, sweetheart, but I had to shock you into realizing it, since my regular words aren't getting through to you." He paused a moment. "Honey, I want you to get over these feelings of insecurity over Pamela. You heard her, Belle. I could be with her right now, and not have to worry about this million-dollar debt. I could move in with her and live happily ever after in that big beautiful mansion, *if,* that's what I wanted. Look around Belle, I'm not with her; I'm here with you. I'm willing to risk everything just to be with you. Doesn't that say it all?" He paused again. "Sweetheart, we'll probably fight about a lot of things down through the years, but let's not waste one minute fighting over Pamela, when there's no reason to do so. It's you I love, Belle, and I always will."

"I'm sorry, Jesse," she muttered sheepishly.

"And, Belle," he continued, determined to put this to rest once and for all. "I don't see beauty when I look at Pamela, I see beauty when I look at you. I'll admit she does have a certain kind of surface beauty, and I was flattered

67

when she flirted with me and told me she wanted me. But I only noticed her because I was mad at you, and wanted to get back at you for the imaginary wrongs you had done to me." He stroked Belle's face. "I don't know why you're so hung up on this. You're much prettier than her and you have something she could never have; an inner beauty that shines through, making you even more beautiful. And, honestly, Belle, I didn't even notice what Pamela was wearing tonight. Why would I want to look at her when the most beautiful girl in the world was standing right beside me."

Belle smiled and turned off the light. Jesse always knew the right words to say. She snuggled close to him. He kissed her and all thoughts of Pamela faded from her mind.

Chapter 9

Bright sunlight shining through the window awoke Brad the next morning. Roseanna was sleeping peacefully beside him. He had talked her into taking a mild sedative last night so she would sleep through the night. He promised to take care of the baby. Little Alex had slept through the night. "That's a bit unusual," he mumbled, looking over at the bassinet. It was gone! The baby was gone! Someone had come in during the night and taken the baby! But how; their alarm system was supposed to be foolproof. Then he remembered---he had left the keys under the mat for Andy and Angelina; they were going to be very late getting there and didn't want to wake anyone. Some one must have been watching, knowing that Roseanna lived there, waiting for their chance to kidnap the baby and hold him for ransom. "Oh, God, please don't let them hurt him, please keep him safe." How was he going to tell Roseanna. She trusted him to take care of the baby, and he had let someone come in and steal him away, right from under his nose. He hurried down the hall.

"Good morning," Andy said, as Brad walked into the kitchen. "I made myself at home, hope you don't mind. Would you like a cup of coffee?"

"The baby's gone," Brad said, hysterically. "Someone came in before you got here and kidnapped him..."

"Calm down," Andy answered. "The baby slept in the room with us. When we got here, he was crying. Angelina peeked in your room and both you and Roseanna were sleeping soundly, so she slipped in and rolled his bassinet out of the room, changed him and fed him, then took him to our room with us," he explained. "We weren't thinking about how alarmed you'd be when you woke up and he was gone."

Brad sank down in a chair with sigh of relief. "Thank God," he said. "I've never been more frightened in my life."

"Sorry about that," Andy said, handing him a cup of coffee. "Brad," he added, "while we're alone, I think we need to talk. I want to apologize to you for what happened at the church that night between Roseanna and me."

"There's no need to apologize," Brad told him, a bit tartly. "Roseanna and I have worked through all of that..."

"I know," Andy interrupted, "but it's still there between you and me. I'm so ashamed. I didn't go there that night with thoughts of anything like that happening. It was a terrible mistake and I take all the blame for it; knowing the way I felt about Roseanna, I never should have met her like that," he continued. "I violated you, Brad, by kissing your wife that way, and I am so very sorry. I have always admired you; first, from the way that Roseanna and all the folks who knew you felt about you; and then from my own observations after I met you. I couldn't believe that I lost control the way I did, or that I had so little respect for the wedding vows between Roseanna and you. I asked God to forgive me that night before I left the church, and He did. Now, I'm asking for your forgiveness, but I'll understand if you can't give it. I hope you can, because I want us to be close, like brothers, the way you and Jesse are. Do you think that's possible?"

"I'm going to be completely honest with you," Brad answered. "I do have qualms about you even though I know there's no reason to do so. I know Roseanna loves me and you love Angelina, so I'm trying with all my might to put these feelings behind me; but it's not that easy; it may take awhile." He hesitated as if trying to decide whether to tell Andy the thoughts he had about the baby. "I have something to confess to you," he finally said. "When we found out that Roseanna had gotten pregnant while we were at the cabin, the devil filled my mind with suspicions about whom the father was. You and Roseanna had been together in the church only a couple of days before we were at the cabin, and I wasn't completely convinced that Roseanna would tell me if something more had happened between the two of you, and I thought if the baby was born with blonde hair..."

"He's got a head full of blonde hair," Andy gasped, "that doesn't mean...Brad, we didn't..."

"I know," Brad said, "but, you can imagine how I felt when I saw all that blonde hair. Then, my mother called and told me it was a family tradition that the Lefourche men are born with blonde hair, so, I want to apologize to you, Andy, for having those doubts about you and Roseanna. I'd like for us to work on being friends, too, so let's put all this behind us and start over." He extended his hand.

Andy shook his hand vigorously. "Now, I feel like I'm really a part of this wonderful family."

Late that afternoon, Andy had steaks on the grill, as well as hot dogs and hamburgers for the kids. Angelina had potatoes baking in the oven, Belle made a big salad, and mama and grandma had brought dessert. All of them hovered over Roseanna making sure she didn't lift a finger to do anything. They had all met Cassie and was doing everything they could to make her feel welcome. The whole family was there, except daddy. He refused to be in the same house with Jesse.

"I'm sorry, honey," mama said, putting her arm around Belle. "You know how your daddy is when someone hurts one of his girls. He doesn't forgive easily and he certainly doesn't forget."

"I'm going over and talk to him," Belle said. "I'm going to straighten him out about Jesse." She got in her car and pulled out on the highway.

"Where's Belle going?" Jesse asked, walking in just as she drove away.

"She's going over to talk to her daddy," mama answered. "She's got a few things to say to him about the way he's treating you."

"She's in no shape to talk to him now," Jesse fretted. "She'll say things she doesn't mean. I've got to stop her, but I'll need a car."

"Take mine," Brad said. "Do you want me to come with you?"

"No, she might think we're ganging up on her," Jesse answered. "Just whisper a prayer."

Belle was fuming when she walked into the house. "Daddy, I want to talk to you about Jesse."

Ellis LeBlanc turned to face his daughter. "Baby Girl, I'm happy to see you, but I refuse to talk about that low-down husband of yours." He pulled her into his arms and started to kiss her.

She yanked free of his grasp. "Daddy, I came here hoping to make peace with you, but I see that was a mistake. I've got a few things to say to you, then as far as I'm concerned, I don't have a father anymore."

"Belle, you don't mean that," he said, a pleading look in his eyes.

Tears were in her eyes. "Daddy, I thought you, of all people, would forgive Jesse. After all, you did the same thing to your family, only worse. I want you to know that when Jesse was away from us, he put most of his earnings each week into my checking account for the kids and me to live on. Even though he wasn't living at home, he still took care of us. That's more than you can say, daddy. You left us with nothing, no money, no food, nothing. You didn't look back. You never sent money; you just didn't care."

Belle was crying as she lashed out in anger. "Don't you dare talk about Jesse when he is much more of a loving man than you!"

Jesse ran in and took her in his arms. He looked at Ellis. "I'm sorry, sir," he said. "She didn't mean those things; this has been rough on her and I take all the blame for that."

"Jesse, don't you dare stick up for him!" Belle screamed. "I won't allow him to do this to you."

"Sweetheart, I understand where your father is coming from," he said tenderly, holding her in his arms. "When Annie grows up, if some man did to her what I've done to you, I'd probably kill him with my bare hands." He turned to Ellis again. "Sir, I want to tell you how sorry I am about these past months. I hurt Belle deeply, and I will have to live with that every day of my life. I'm going to spend the rest of my life trying to make it up to her and the kids, and I'd like to have your blessing. I want all of us to be a family again. I realize I'm the one who tore this family apart and I want to do my part to put it back together, so will you forgive me?"

Ellis lowered his gaze. "She's right, Jesse," he said, tears of guilt and remorse flowing down his face, "I am not fit to be a father." He put his hand on his daughter's arm. "Belle, I have no right to your love or respect. I have failed you miserably. I don't deserve your forgiveness, but I am so sorry for what I did to you all those years ago, and what I've done to Jesse. I'm just a worthless, no good…"

"No, daddy, I didn't mean it," she cried. "I love you. You're a good daddy. Please forgive me for lashing out like that." She ran into his arms.

He put his arm around her and kissed her, tears still running down his face. "I love you, Baby Girl," he said, and putting his other arm around Jesse, he pulled him close. "Jesse, please forgive me. I had no right to treat you that way."

"It's forgotten, sir," Jesse said. "Thank you for accepting me back into the family. You're the only real father I've ever had. Your love has meant so much to me. My father never loved me; the only thing I remember about him was his abuse. I didn't know what a father's love could be like, until I met you."

Ellis LeBlanc broke down and wept. "Jesse, you're like a son to me, too. I guess one reason I was so angry with you was that I loved you so much and you let me down. Perhaps, I saw some of my qualities coming out in you and it scared me. Belle told me she was at fault too, but I couldn't see that. I know now, that the devil was working against you and Belle; and I also know you're a fine young man and I'm glad my daughter has someone like you taking care of her."

The three of them stood there in each other's embrace while tears of refreshing ran down their faces; tears that would erase hateful words that had been spoken; guilt that had been dealt with; and anger that had been shut up for much too long.

"We'd better get going before the others eat all the food and we don't get any," Ellis LeBlanc remarked. "Belle, you ride with your husband and I'll drive your car."

After they had finished supper and the kitchen was spic and span, they sent the kids to play in Isabelle's playroom, then, Andy called the family together. He told them all the things that had happened to Cassie, her mother being carried away by the police, Cassie going to look for her and ending up on the streets, how Duke was there and took care of her, and then, how she ended up in the clutches of that horrible man who said he had bought her and she belonged to him, how she managed to get away from him, and how Andy came along just in time to save her.

"She will be in a lot of danger if she stays in Friend's Harbor; that man and his friends will be looking for her 'cause she can identify him," he explained, "so, we had to

74

find a safe place for her, and Kent suggested we bring her here. I was hesitant, knowing the danger this could put all of you in, but…"

Angelina broke in before he could finish. "I told him that my family would want to make sure that Cassie was safe, that you would insist she stay here out of harms way."

"What are the chances of us being in danger if she stays here?" Ellis asked, concerned about the safety of his family.

"Kent doesn't believe there will be any danger; as long as no one associates Cassie with the bayou, you'll all be safe. And, there's no way they could do that, because no one knows that Cassie ended up with us, so there will be no reason to suspect that she's here, even if they know where this place is. The chances of them tracking her here is less than one in a million."

"Kent knows his business, and if he says we'll be safe, then I think we have to trust his judgment," Roseanna said.

Brad nodded. "I'm willing to put my life in his hands. Kent wouldn't put this family in danger, so I think we ought to take Cassie into our homes and let her know that's she's safe here with us. What do you think, Mama?"

"I don't know how we could turn the child away," Mama said. "I would love to have another little girl to take care of; all my girls are practically grown. What about it, honey?" She looked at her husband.

He was quiet for a moment. "Just how widespread is this slavery ring? Is it contained just to the area around Friend's Harbor?"

"They don't know for sure," Andy replied, "but, they believe it is operating in a big portion of the country. That's why we're taking precautions. First, Steve, we'll need your help. It won't be safe for her to go to school, because of the records they would need…"

75

"No problem," Steve interrupted, "I'll come over everyday after school and teach her. I can get the materials she needs without raising suspicions."

"And, Jesse, after what she's been through, she's going to need some big time counseling..."

"I can take care of that," Jesse answered before Andy had a chance to ask.

"Okay, I believe that covers all the bases here," Andy said. "Angelina and I will be working closely with the FBI to try to find her mother..."

"Won't that be dangerous?" Ellis blurted out.

"We shouldn't be in any danger as long as they don't associate us with Cassie, and there's no way they can do that. The man that was chasing her ran away without getting a look at me or my car, so they don't have a clue that we have ever met her."

"Be careful," Ellis warned, worried that Angelina and Andy might be in grave danger.

"We will, daddy," Angelina promised. "Does this mean Cassie can stay?"

"I vote yes," he said, "what about the rest of you?" They all nodded their heads. It was official. Cassie was staying.

Duke had searched the last two days for Cassie. What happened to her? Did she get lost trying to find her way back to the warehouse? He had to find her, and soon. She couldn't survive out here on the streets by herself. Even more troubling thoughts filled his mind. What if that man was a pervert and had hurt Cassie? "I didn't feel right about her going off with him. Why didn't I stop her?" he mumbled over the lump in his throat. "I'm sorry, Little Flower, this is all my fault, and I won't give up 'til I find you." But he knew that with each passing day his chances of finding her grew slimmer. "If they hurt you, I'll find them and make them pay," he vowed, tears misting his eyes, as he thought about what could have happened to her.

"Hey, kid, do you mind if I bunk down here for the night?" a man's voice asked, interrupting his thoughts.

Duke swore under his breath. He didn't like strangers, and especially those who invaded his space. He turned and looked at the man standing in the doorway of the warehouse. He was unkempt, as were most people out here on the streets. He was tall with a straggly beard, and graying hair that fell loose down around his shoulders. He carried a big backpack.

"I-I don't know," Duke stuttered nervously. "I usually go it alone…"

"I won't cramp your style," the man promised. "I just need a place to stay for a few days, then, I'll be moving on. I have some food in my backpack and money to buy more, and, I'll gladly share it with you if you will let me stay here."

The man was bigger than him, so Duke didn't see that he had a choice. "Okay," he said, "just don't crowd me." He was hungry. It had been a couple of days since he ate. He didn't have the heart to go to McDonald's without Cassie there to go with him, and he hadn't felt up to eating anyway.

The man pulled a box of fried chicken out of his backpack, along with potatoes, slaw and some biscuits. "I bought this at that chicken place down the street, so it's still good and hot." He took some of the food and handed the rest to Duke.

"Thanks, mister," Duke said, digging into the food with a fury. It had been a long time since he had tasted anything this good.

"Call me Tom," the man said. "What do I call you?"

"Duke," the boy answered, between bites. He wondered where the man got the money for such a fine feast, but he didn't ask.

"I live on the streets, but I work enough to buy food," the man said, as if reading Duke's thoughts. "I'm sorta of a vagabond; don't like to stay in one place too long, so I take odd jobs in the towns I land in. I'll look for something here for a couple of days, and then I'll move on."

"Do you hop freight trains?"

"I don't really like trains," Tom told him. "I hitch rides from truckers; they are good company and don't ask too many questions."

They finished eating and then dusk was falling so they made ready for bed while it was still enough light to see.

Tom lay there in the darkness thinking about this kid he'd been sent here to protect. Was he a part of the slavery ring? Did he deliberately send Cassie into the clutches of that man? He had to find out if Duke was a part of it, or if he was just a kid that was in more trouble than he even knew about. He'd gain his confidence and get him talking. He could learn a lot by just observing him. He didn't get very many assignments that involved kids. He thought of another case, a few years back, where he had gone undercover to prove that a man was molesting his two stepdaughters; but, before he could get the proof that he was looking for, he caught the man dealing drugs, and Carl Jenkins was sent to prison for many years to come. He remembered how good it felt to know he had saved two young girls from a fate worse than death; and he wondered how they were doing. It felt good knowing he had helped give them a chance at a good life. He closed his eyes and silently wished that this case turned out as well as that one did.

Chapter 10

"I want a baby," Angelina declared as she sat leaned back in Andy's arms on their way back to Friends Harbor.

"What brought this on?" Andy asked, stoking her hair.

"I guess the main thing was when I held baby Alex; but, also, I saw the look in your eyes when you looked at Will. I know it must have been hard on you, thinking that you were going to be his father, and then in one instant losing him like that. I know you still love him. I could see the hurt even though you tried to hide it."

"You don't miss anything, do you?" he answered. "For the first few hours of his life he was my son, and no one could have loved a baby more than I loved him. But that's in the past, and, I want to look to the future. I want us to have a baby, but because we want to; not to help me get over the pain of losing Will."

"Honey, I'll admit that's the main reason that I want to have a baby now. I want to help erase the hurt from your eyes and fill the void that losing Will left inside you. I can't bear to see you hurting like that..."

"Angelina," he cried, his eyes misting, "You'd get pregnant and go through all that suffering just to take the hurt out of my heart?"

"My darling, I'd do anything for you."

He pulled her close and kissed her. "I'm the luckiest man on this planet having you for my wife. I love you sweetheart, but I can't let you do this."

"Why not?"

"It's not the right time," he said. "In a few years, when your schooling is behind you…"

"No," she interrupted. "I don't want to wait years before starting a family. I want a baby now."

"What about your career? Are you willing to give that up?"

"No, but I can be a mother and a doctor at the same time," she answered. "When I held little Alex in my arms and gave him his bottle, it was the most wonderful feeling, and I knew I wanted a baby of my own."

"Honey, you'll be out of school in a couple months or so, but what about your internship. That's long hours and lots of hard work. Do you think you can handle that, and a baby, too?"

"I'm not saying it will be easy," she said, then paused and looked at her husband. "You do want a baby, don't you?"

"Sweetheart, I'd love to have a baby with you, but not until you're absolutely sure that you are ready."

"Oh, I'm ready," she said, "and, as soon as I graduate we can start making plans for our little son or daughter."

"I think we should wait until this slavery ring business is all behind us, then we can talk about starting a family. There would be too much stress on you right now, not to mention the possible danger."

"You're right, of course," she said, "so we'll put our plans on hold for a while." She rested quietly in his arms as the plane's motor drummed out a steady rhythm, soaring through the darkened skies, taking them closer to home, and, to whatever awaited them in the days ahead.

The man called Tom heard the boy stirring around. He opened his eyes just enough to see what was going on. Duke was getting ready to leave. He pretended to still be asleep, so the boy wouldn't suspect that he was watching him. As soon as Duke walked out the door, Tom jumped up, slipped his shoes on, and hurried over to the window. He got there just in time to see Duke turn left into the alley. He picked up his backpack and followed, at a safe distance, so Duke wouldn't see him. This kid was a tough one. He'd been with him for the most part of two days and he didn't know anymore about him, now, than he did when he first got here. He couldn't come right out and ask him about Cassie; that would give him away. He couldn't let the boy out of his sight, not only in order to protect him, but also to find out if he was a part of the slavery ring. "I sure hope he isn't," he muttered under his breath.

Duke walked to the alley where he had first met Cassie. Maybe, she would come back here, since it was familiar to her. After finding no sign of her, he retraced all the places they had been together, hoping to get a glimpse of her. Nothing. Guilt filled him; fear gnawed at his insides. Something awful had happened to her, and it was his fault. He'd find the man he had talked to on the streets that day, the one who had hired Cassie. He'd beat the truth out of him. He wouldn't stop until he found her. He walked the streets for hours, then, finally headed back to the warehouse. He made sure no one was around, then, falling down on the mattress, he let go of all the hurting and pain inside him.

Tom walked in and heard Duke crying. He hurried over to him. "What's wrong, kid. Can I help?"

Duke would usually have been mortified if someone caught him in tears, but there was something in Tom's voice that reminded him of Gus; something that told him he could trust the man; and he did need to talk about Cassie. He nodded his head and told him the whole story. "I know something awful has happened to her and it's all my fault," he cried. "What if they've..." he couldn't finish the sentence, knowing what happens to young girls when that kind of men gets hold of them.

Tom put his arms around the young boys shoulders. He knew now that Duke was in no way connected to the slavery ring. He breathed a sigh of relief. "Don't beat up on yourself," he said compassionately, wishing he could tell him that Cassie was safe; but someone else would tell him that. His job here was almost finished. He would make a phone call to the chief and they would pick Duke up and take him somewhere far away from here where he would be safe. Until then he would watch over him in case some of the members of the ring found his hiding place.

"Here's a hamburger and some fries," he said, handing a bag to Duke. "I've got to step outside for a moment, but you go ahead and start eating." He walked out of the warehouse, took his cell phone from his pocket, and dialed.

Later, that night, Duke was sleeping peacefully when all at once someone grabbed him and pulled him to his feet. He fought with all his might, trying to wrench free of the masked man's grasp. He called out to Tom for help, then, he saw another man in a mask holding a gun on him, ordering him not to move. The man kept the gun aimed at Tom until they got Duke in the car and started driving away. Duke looked back, and in the faint light from the car's taillights, saw Tom running out the door, with a look of panic on his face.

Andy and Angelina got home late on Sunday night. He would wait and call Kent in the morning and give him a rundown on how things went with Cassie. Both he and Angelina were tired to the bone and needed to get to sleep. They had barely gotten to bed when the phone rang.

"I know it's an hour later there," Kent apologized, "but I couldn't wait to find out how things went with Cassie. Did she stay with your folks?"

"Yeah," Andy said, trying to suppress a yawn, but not succeeding. "They were more than happy to keep her there with them."

"Ellis went along with it?"

"He had a few questions concerning the safety of his family, but they all trust your judgment, and convinced him that there was no danger in her being there," Andy explained. "Have you heard anymore?"

"Only that we have a man on the streets with Duke, so he's safe now; and, even though it's hush-hush, you can tell Cassie when you talk to her."

"Good," Andy said. "It will ease her mind and hopefully help her to adjust to her new surroundings."

They talked on for a few minutes then said goodbye, with Kent promising to call as soon as he learned anything new.

Andy went to bed with a relieved mind, knowing that both Cassie and Duke were safe.

Meanwhile, in another part of town, in a deserted warehouse, an undercover agent was desperately trying to come to grips with what had just happened. How could he let them take the boy? He had been trained to be on guard at all times, so something like that wouldn't happen; and it never had before. Should he have put up a fight instead of just letting the men take Duke? He had reacted the way he'd been trained, not putting the young boy's life in danger by resisting. But, had he put him in more danger by letting those people get their hands on him. The FBI would be here soon to pick Duke up; he'd better fill them in on what happened. He dialed his cell phone.

Chapter 11

"You stop this car! Let me out of here right now!" Duke demanded, fighting the man sitting beside him in the back seat, with all the strength he had. Then, it dawned on him; these were probably the same men who took Cassie, and they were out to get him. "What did you do to her? If you hurt her, I'll…"

"Relax, kid," the man sitting in the front seat, seemingly the boss of the operation, stated. "We're the good guys," he continued, showing Duke his FBI badge, "and your little friend is safe. She got away from the man who took her, and she is in a place far away from here."

"Where is she?"

"I can't tell you that, but I assure you, she is safe."

"Did that man hurt her?"

"No, she got away from him before he could do anything to her. She's plenty worried about you, so we will let her know that you are safe, too." He then told Duke about the slavery ring and why it was necessary to get him off the streets.

"You won't send me back home, will you?"

Chief Bristol could hear the panic in his voice. "No, son, we wouldn't send you home, even if we knew where you lived…" The ringing of his cell phone interrupted him. "Hello," he said.

"Chief, it's me!" the voice on the other end of the line yelled. "They got him! Two masked men came in and took him at gunpoint."

The chief laughed. "Relax, that was us, we've got him…"

"But why did you do it that way? Why didn't you let me in on your little plan?"

"It had to look convincing, in case someone was watching..."

"What if I had resisted?"

"We wouldn't have shot you," the chief said, laughing again. "And, I knew you were too well trained to put up a fight and risk the boy's life."

"You came all the way here to handle this personally?" the undercover agent asked.

"Yeah, we didn't know if we could trust the locals," Chief Bristol told him. "We don't know how widespread this ring is, or who all is involved, so we didn't want to take any chances with the boy's safety. We flew in on a private jet. We're on our way back to the airport now. Your assignment is finished here, so you can leave when you're ready, and, you have a few days before your next assignment, so go somewhere and relax."

"I'll catch the first plane out tomorrow. It's been a while since I saw my family, so I think I'll go home for a few days."

"You did a great job here," the chief said. "Thanks to you, the boy is safe and we know he's not a part of this. Have a nice vacation and I'll see you in a week or so."

Cassie's thoughts were on the past few days as she walked along the bayou. "Mama," she whispered, a tear sliding down her face. She felt so far away from her mother. She liked all the people here, and they had been good to her, but she wished she were back in Friend's Harbor, back on the streets with Duke. At least there she felt close to her mother. And, what about Duke, what was all of this doing to him? Andy said they would send someone in to protect him, but what if it was already too late? What if those people had already found him, what would they do to him---he could identify the man he had talked to on the street----the man who had hired her. She found a spot underneath a big oak tree, fell down on the big log that was lying there, and sobbed as the hopelessness of it all engulfed her. She remembered what mama had told her about the Baby, and of her conversation with Mr. Andy, yesterday, right before he left to go to the airport and back home to Friend's Harbor.

"Mr. Andy, have you ever heard of a wonderful little Baby that was born a long time ago, who has powers so great that he can do anything, and a love so big that he will help anyone who needs him?"

"Yes, I've heard of Him, Cassie," Andy replied with a smile.

"Do you think he really will---help anyone, that is?"

Andy nodded, wondering where this was going. "Why do you ask?"

"Mama always told me if I ever got in trouble, just find the Baby and he would help me. That day, when that man was chasing me, I asked the Baby to help me, but then you came along and I didn't need his help. Do you believe he would have helped me if you hadn't come along?"

Andy took her in his arms. "Honey, I know for a fact it was the Baby who helped you that day. He did it by making sure I was there at exactly the right time. I wasn't supposed to be on that street; I had turned onto it by mistake and only realized a minute or so before I heard you scream, that I was on the wrong street; so you see He had me there at the right place before you even called on Him."

"He can do that?" she asked, puzzled about the whole thing.

"Honey, He can do anything, and I wish I had time to tell you all about the Baby, but my pilot has already filed flight plans so we have to leave right now in order to get to the airport in time," Andy explained. "The folks here can tell you all about the Baby, especially Brad..."

"The preacher?" she asked in surprise. "The Baby has something to do with church?"

86

"He has everything to do with church," Andy answered, kissing her on the forehead.

"Cassie."

She was jolted back to the present as she heard her name being called. She jumped up just as Ellis LeBlanc came walking up.

"I should have known you'd be here," he remarked. "This is my daughter's special place, and sooner or later everyone finds their way to this spot."

"Which daughter?" she asked. "You have so many."

He laughed. "Six to be exact," he answered. "This is Roseanna's special place. I used to bring her here when she was small. This is where I taught her how to play the guitar and sing."

"I can't believe I met the real Roseanna," Cassie said, musingly. "She's mama's favorite singer. She used to listen to her tapes all the time and she'd sing along with her. Mama has a good voice." She paused a moment. "Do you think they will find my mother, Mr. LeBlanc?"

Kent and Chief Bristol are two of the best there is, and they won't stop until they find her," he assured her.

"What if she's, a, dead?" Cassie could hardly get the word out. "What if they killed her?"

"Kent and the chief are both convinced that she is still alive," he said. "It would draw too much attention to the people who took her if she turned up dead."

"I hope they're right."

"I trust their judgment," he told her, then, added, "Kent called a few minutes ago. The FBI has Duke in their custody. They are taking him to a place where he will be safe. Kent didn't say where they were taking him, but they wanted you to know he is safe, now. Those people can't touch him."

Tears misted her eyes as a load lifted from her shoulders. Duke was safe and he knew that she was too, so he wouldn't have to fret over her anymore. "Thank you for coming out here and telling me this, Mr. LeBlanc," she said, giving him a grateful hug.

"Steve also called," he told her. "He will be over around four this afternoon to start teaching you. He said to try and remember the last things you studied before you ran away."

Today was Belle's first day back to work in over two weeks. First, Roseanna had been rushed to the hospital, where she and the baby almost died; then Belle had come down with the flu and had been in bed for almost a week. She had not talked to Lance since the day he had gotten back into town, and had called to tell her the news of his engagement to Sara. He didn't know that Jesse was back home.

"Are you all right?" he asked when she walked into the office. "Are you sure you feel up to being here?"

She nodded. "Do we have time to talk?" she asked, wanting to fill him in on how things were going in her life.

"Of course," he said. "Close the door and sit down. Is this about Jesse? What's he done now?"

She smiled. "Jesse is back home. We worked things out and we're back together for good."

"Belle, that's great news," he said, "if you're sure this is what you want; if you're happy."

"I'm very happy having Jesse back home, and life would be perfect for us if not for Pamela..."

"Jesse's not still seeing her," he blurted out.

"No, of course not, but that doesn't mean she's out of our lives. She came by the house Friday night and dropped a bombshell on us..."

"She's pregnant!" he exclaimed. "Belle, I'm so sorry."

"No, that's not it," Belle explained and told him the whole story about the million dollar loan on the house.

"That conniving…" he cut his sentence short, not wanting to use that kind of language in front of Belle. He took her hands. "Belle, I'll give you the money…"

"That's not an option," she said, shaking her head. "Roseanna and Andy have already offered. Jesse won't accept money that we could never pay back. We all tried to come up with a plan to stop her, but so far we've come up with zilch."

"That's because you're all too pure minded," he said. "You've got to be devious to outwit someone like Pamela. Let me think this over. Maybe, I can figure out a way to get you out of this mess."

Dear, sweet Lance. Always watching out for her. She leaned over and kissed him. "Thanks, Lance, you're the best friend ever."

"Well, if I don't come up with something, you won't end up on the streets. You can move into the guesthouse on Grandmother's estate; it's a big house with plenty of room for all of you. I would offer to let you move into the main house but I know Jesse would never go for that."

"Thanks again, Lance," she said. "Now, I want to hear all about Sara and you."

Later, that day, Lance pushed the buzzer to Belle's office. "I've got it," he exclaimed. "I've come up with a way to get that hussy off your backs for good."

Belle rushed to his office. "What's your plan?" she asked excitedly.

"Either Roseanna or I will loan you the money to pay off the debt…"

"But, Jesse will never go along with that…"

"Just keep quiet and hear me out," he said. "When Jesse pays off the loan, he can do whatever he wants to with his half of the house, right?"

She nodded. "I'm sure that's the way it would work," she said, not seeing the significance of that.

"Okay, he borrows the money, pays off the balloon note, then contacts a realtor about putting his half of the house on the market. He will then go to Pamela, tell her his plans and offer her first option to buy him out. If she refuses, he calls the realtor and tells him to start showing the house. I think she will change her mind once people start tromping through her home. I don't believe she will want anyone invading her privacy."

"Lance, you're wonderful," she exclaimed, hugging him. "I'm going to call Jesse right now and tell him the news."

"No, call him and tell him to take the rest of the day off and meet you at home," Lance suggested. "You can tell him the good news in person, and then go out on the town and celebrate your victory together."

"I'm going to call Roseanna and tell her. She will be so excited, and she'll want to get right to work getting the funds together," Belle remarked with a renewed spark in her voice. "You're a genius, Lance. I can hardly wait to see Pamela's face when she learns that Jesse has come up with the money; and that he's put his half of the house on the market. How can we ever thank you?"

"Just be happy, Belle," he said, kissing her fondly. "That's all I've ever wanted for you."

"Now, thanks to you, we will be rid of Pamela, once and for all," Belle commented. "And, that, my dear friend, makes me very happy."

Belle's heart was light as she left the office and drove home to meet Jesse; to tell him the news that would set them free from the clutches of Pamela for good. At least that was the way it was supposed to turn out.

Chapter 12

Today was the day; the day that Belle and Jesse would get rid of Pamela once and for all.

Brad and Roseanna came into town early, and by noon Jesse had a cashiers check for one million dollars to pay off the loan. Jesse personally handed the check to the representative at the loan company, then went out to lunch with Belle, Roseanna and Brad while the necessary papers were being filed. A couple of hours later Jesse walked out of the mortgage company with the legal papers that confirmed his ownership of half of the mansion. He went back to his office and Brad and Roseanna went home with Belle.

"I positively drool every time I think of the look on Pamela's face when we break the news to her," Belle commented to Roseanna as they sat in the den of her house; the house she and Jesse would get to keep, now that the loan was paid and everything was legal. "I want to be the one to tell her, I think it will be more of a bitter pill to swallow coming from me."

"I wish I could be there to see that," Roseanna said, savoring the sweet taste of revenge that her sister was going to feel when she finally put one over on Pamela.

Brad walked in from the kitchen in time to hear the comments. He shook his head. "Revenge is never as sweet as it is made out to be," he stated and sat down on the couch beside his wife.

"I know I'm supposed to love my enemies and all that, but, I haven't gotten there with Pamela yet, and I'm not sure I ever will," Belle said, picking up on the message that Brad wanted to convey to her.

"Sweetheart, just be careful," Brad said gently. "Don't put more emphasis on getting even with Pamela than you do on winning a victory over the devil." He knew what Belle had been through, and he could understand how much she wanted to make Pamela pay for all the heartache she'd caused her family, but, he also knew what vengeance against others could do to your own heart.

"We've got to be going," Roseanna commented, looking at her watch. "We've got to pick Isabelle up from school, and we've got just about enough time to get there." She leaned over and kissed Belle. "Give it to her good," she whispered, so Brad wouldn't hear.

"Thanks, sis, for making all of this possible," Belle said, and waved goodbye to them as they walked out the door.

A few minutes later the phone rang. It was Jesse.

"Honey, I called Pamela's office to tell her we were coming over tonight. Her secretary told me she had gotten ill and had gone home for the day. I've seen my last patient today and I'd like to get this over with, so can you go now?"

"I'll need a few minutes to get ready," she answered, and hung up the phone. She had to look just right for this visit to Pamela's. It was pay back time. Pamela had gone home sick so she would probably look a mess. Belle smiled. This time she would catch Pamela off guard and hopefully she'd be wearing a ratty old housecoat or something even worse. "Revenge is sweet," she muttered as she rummaged through her closet for just the right outfit to wear. She chose a bright red silk dress with a slightly plunging neckline; she usually wore a scarf at the neckline, but not this time; instead she fastened the locket that Jesse had given her at Christmas around her neck. She applied make-up that complimented the dress, then, pulled her hair up slightly and secured it with pins, making sure they couldn't be seen. She used the curling iron on the ends, and around her face, letting wisps of hair fall down around her temples.

She pulled on long dark stockings and slipped her feet into a pair of high-heeled black patent shoes. She dabbed perfume on her wrists and behind her ears just as Jesse walked in the front door. She ran downstairs and into his arms.

He let out a whistle. "Wow, you're dressed to kill," he said, looking her over and then giving her a big kiss. "I feel underdressed. Should I put on a tux?"

She laughed. "It's pay back time," she said. "Pamela is going to know how it feels to get caught off guard, and I hope she looks perfectly awful."

He shook his head. "No matter what she's wearing; in that outfit you have on, you're going to make her look like a toad," he said, kissing her again. "You look absolutely amazing."

A few minutes later, they pulled into the driveway of the mansion. Jesse got out of the car and started to open the door for Belle.

"You go on ahead," she said. "I want to make a grand entrance."

He walked up to the door and rang the doorbell. He waited a moment, than rang it again. "Pamela, it's Jesse, let me in," he called.

Pamela opened the door, threw her arms around Jesse and kissed him. "I knew you'd come home to me," she exclaimed, kissing him again.

He stepped out of her arms just as Belle walked up. "Hello, Pamela," she said, smiling smugly.

"What are you doing here?" Pamela asked angrily.

"I want to give you this," Belle said, handing her a copy of the loan papers. "See, it says right there, 'paid in full'," she gloated, pointing to the words.

"But how?" Pamela stammered. "You don't have that kind of money."

"But we do have rich relatives," Belle informed her.

"Jesse would never borrow money that he couldn't pay back," Pamela stuttered.

"You're right, so we had to come up with a way to pay the money back," Belle said, smiling wryly at the other woman. "Honey, you tell her this part."

"Pamela, since I don't have any use for my half of the mansion, I'm going to put it on the market, but, I want to give you the option to buy it before I contact a realtor…"

Her face turned pale and she started to cry. "Jesse, you can't do this to me. We made promises to each other. You belong to me…"

He held out his hand showing her his wedding band. "This is who I belong to," he said. "I will always belong to Belle."

"Jesse, how could you do this?" she cried. "You don't owe her anything; she threw you out, and you came to me. The day you placed a ring on my finger and asked me to be your wife, you broke your commitment to Belle; Jesse, you committed yourself to me."

"You knew I loved Belle."

"Jesse, there's love, and there's commitment. I accepted the commitments you made to me, I didn't insist on your love." Tears filled her eyes. "I was content leaving things the way they were, you and me living together; but your high morals wouldn't let you do that, so you bought this ring and asked me to marry you. You owe me, Jesse. I gave up my lifestyle to please you. You promised that we would have a life together as soon as the divorce was final." She held out her hand. "You placed this ring on my finger the day you gave your wedding band back to Belle. You made commitments to me…"

"Well, I'm not too good at keeping commitments, am I? If I had been, I never would have taken my wedding band off in the first place."

Belle stood there in shock as she saw the size of the diamond on Pamela's finger; it made the diamond on her finger look like a grain of mustard seed.

Pamela started to cry. "Jesse, I trusted you," she sobbed. "I thought you were different from the other men I'd known, the ones who used me through the years. I opened up my heart to you, Jesse, I allowed you inside..." Her eyes rolled back in her head and she toppled forward.

Jesse reached out and caught her. He carried her over to the couch and laid her down. He hurried into the bathroom and came out with a wet towel and a container of smelling salts. He laid the towel on her forehead. "Pamela," he said, gently waving the salts under her nose. "Pamela."

She sputtered and opened her eyes. "Jesse, I'm going to be sick," she cried, jumping up and stumbling to the bathroom.

Jesse ran after her and Belle could hear her heaving as he held on to her.

"How long has it been since you've eaten?" Jesse asked, helping her back to the couch.

She shook her head.

"Have you eaten at all today?"

She shook her head again. "I'm not hungry."

"Well, you're going to eat," he said, and walked into the kitchen. "Pamela, have you moved the crackers," he yelled. "Never mind, I found them." He came back in a few minutes, with a bowl of tomato soup, a plate of crackers and a peanut butter sandwich. "I know you like tomato soup fixed with milk, but I used water instead, because of your upset stomach," he told her as he sat the food down on the table beside the couch. "Now eat." He walked back into the kitchen and brought out another tray with three mugs of coffee. He sat one down on the table for Pamela, handed one to Belle, and holding the other one, he sat down beside Pamela.

Belle sat there taking this all in. Was Pamela really sick or was this a ruse to get Jesse's sympathy? It sure was working. Jesse was rushing to her aid. It was as if the two of them were alone, like she was invisible. Belle couldn't believe what was happening here. She remembered the afternoon that Jesse had come home and they'd gotten back together, how he had fussed over her, and insisted she eat; now, he was fussing over Pamela the same way, and, he didn't seem to notice that she looked a mess.

Belle wished she'd never come here. Things were not working out the way they were supposed to. She'd heard and seen things that she had rather not know, things that Jesse hadn't mentioned. Did he have something to hide?

Pamela finished eating and Jesse carried the dishes into the kitchen, rinsed them and put them in the dishwasher. Then, he came back and sat down on the couch again.

"Are you feeling better?" he asked, taking Pamela's hand.

She nodded, then, burst into tears again. "Jesse, how could you do this to me, after all we've been to each other; how could you even think about selling half of my house to strangers?"

"You backed me into a corner, Pamela," he said as calmly as he could. "You threatened the welfare of my family, and I won't let anyone, not even you, do that. I'm sorry that you got hurt in all of this, but my family comes first, before anyone, and, I am giving you first option to buy it; money won't be a problem for you, so it's really up to you whether or not strangers move in here with you."

"You'll have a check by tomorrow afternoon," she said in a sad, frosty tone. "Now please go and leave me alone."

"Belle, you've been so quiet," Jesse remarked on their way home. Her silence worried him. He thought she would be bubbling over now that they finally had Pamela off their backs. "Honey, is something wrong?"

She shrugged her shoulders, but said nothing.

96

"Sweetheart, you should be celebrating. You got your revenge on Pamela."

"Brad's right," she mumbled, as if talking to herself rather than Jesse. "Revenge is not as sweet as it's made out to be."

He reached over and pulled her close to him. "Talk to me, Belle; tell me what's wrong."

"You gave her a ring? You promised to marry her? You didn't tell me that, Jesse."

"Belle, I only saw you a couple of times after I gave her the ring; the night we bought the Christmas tree and again on Christmas Day, and those times were so special to me, I didn't want to spoil them by mentioning it."

"You told me you detested her, but at some point you must have loved her, to ask her to become your wife." A tear slid down Belle's face as she faced the possibility that Jesse might have lied to her.

"Honey, let me explain," he said, pleadingly. "I was so confused then; I thought I had lost you forever. When I was sober, my thoughts were on you and the kids, and the precious love I had thrown away. The only way I could put these thoughts out of my mind was by drinking, so that's what I did. Every day after work, as soon as I got home, I'd pick up a bottle and I didn't stop until I was too drunk to think anymore. So, you see, Belle, the decisions I made then, were not rational ones; and, it was one of those times that I asked her to marry me. The divorce hearing was coming up, and I believed that you and I would be divorced when it was over, and I would never see you or the kids again. Without you in my life nothing mattered anyway, so I bought the ring, expecting to marry Pamela right after the hearing. Thank God, it didn't turn out that way." He hesitated a moment. "Belle, when I told you I hated every minute I spent with her, I wasn't actually lying. After I left her and made things right with God, I looked back on my life with her and it made me sick to think about it. But,

97

while I was with her, there were moments between us that were good. I'm sorry I misled you, baby."

"Have you misled me about other things, Jesse?" she asked. "Your true feelings for Pamela, maybe?"

"Belle, no," he answered with a worried look on his face. "What's bothering you honey? What did I do to make you doubt me like this?"

"Jesse, back there at Pamela's, it was like you were at home. When she fainted, you knew exactly where things were in the bathroom, and when you so lovingly fixed the food for her, you knew your way around the kitchen."

Jesse winched. Belle hit too close to the truth; back at Pamela's house, for a while it was as if he were at home, alone with Pamela, as memories of the good times he'd shared with her tried to surface. Those feelings scared him. He wanted to take Belle in his arms and tell her the truth; but their marriage was hanging by a delicate thread, so for now he had keep to keep quiet; someday, maybe he would tell her, but not today.

"Belle, I lived there for months, so of course, I would know my way around. I don't understand---why does that bother you?"

Belle was crying now. "Today, for the first time, I realized that you lived together like a real couple, doing all the little things that families do; you sat across the table from each other at meal time, you cleaned up the kitchen together, your toothbrushes hung side by side in the bathroom, your dirty clothes were in the same hamper; you must have held her in your arms, planning the future you would have together, as man and wife. I thought your relationship with her was just about sex..."

"We didn't spend all our time in bed!" he lashed out angrily. "So, that's what you think of me, huh? You think I would use Pamela, or any other woman, that way? How dare you insult me like that!" He moved his arm from around her and stared straight ahead.

Belle scooted to the other side of the car, as far away from him as possible. "The ring, Jesse, where did you get the money for the ring?" she snapped angrily. "That thing has a diamond big enough to choke a horse; it must have cost thousands of dollars, and I know you didn't have that kind of money."

Jesse sat in silence. He couldn't tell Belle where he got the money for the ring; she'd never forgive him, so silence was his only hope.

"Jesse, I'll ask you again, where did you get the money for the ring?"

He had to be careful how he answered her; their future depended on it. There was only one way to handle it, and he knew she would be mad at him forever, but at least it wouldn't hurt her as much as the truth would. "Belle, I don't believe that it's any of your business how I paid for the ring since we were separated then, and on the verge of getting a divorce." His voice was firm. "So, let's drop it; this conversation is over."

She quickly wiped away a tear that tried to roll down her cheek. She was glad the conversation was over 'cause she was tired of listening to his phony explanations.

Chapter 13

"Belle, can you hold the fort down for a few days," Lance asked the next morning when she got to work.

"Sure, what's up?"

"I'm going to Nashville," he explained. "Sara received a letter from a lawyer in Atlanta asking her to come to his office. Said it a matter of grave importance. She has no idea what it could be, so I'm going with her in case it's bad news."

"You don't have to worry about things here," she said. "When are you leaving?"

"I'm on my way out the door now. She has to be there tomorrow, so I've chartered a jet, and I'm on my way to the airport. We'll go to Nashville and pick up Sara, then on to Atlanta," he explained. "Thanks, Belle, for being here for me.

"Always," she said, giving him a kiss. "Give Sara my love."

Sara was nervous the next morning as they walked into the lawyer's office. Lance walked up to the desk.

"Sara Benson is here," he told the receptionist.

"Follow me," she said, taking them to a room. "You can wait in here. Mr. Owens will be with you in a few minutes."

Sara paced, unable to stop the queasy feeling in the pit of her stomach. What was this all about?

Lance walked over to her and took her in his arms. "It's okay, honey," he said.

She shook her head. "Why did he insist I come all the way to Atlanta? Why couldn't he just tell me on the phone? It must be something really bad…"

"Sometimes it's good news, Sara," Lance said, trying to put her fears at rest. "Do you have any rich relatives?"

"In my family? I don't think so," she answered. "No, this is something else, and I'm almost afraid to find out what it is."

The attorney walked in. "I'm Daniel Owens. I sent you the letter…"

"What's this all about?" Sara blurted out.

"It's a private matter," the attorney said, looking at Lance.

"This is Lance Pecot, my fiancé," Sara explained. "I'd like for him to stay, if that's okay."

"Certainly. This concerns him too since you two are going to be married." He motioned to the two chairs setting in front of his desk. "Have a seat." He pulled some papers out of a file that was lying on his desk.

"What could you possibly want with me?" Sara asked anxiously.

"You are Sara Benson, right?"

She nodded. "Yes, I'm Sara Benson."

"Miss Benson, you had a baby about nine years ago, right?"

"That's right, a little girl." Sara gasped. "Has something happened to her?" The color drained from her face. Lance reached over and took her hand. "Please tell me my baby is okay."

"You're little girl is fine," the lawyer assured her.

"You know where she is," Sara stated weakly. "Is she happy? Is she well?" By this time Sara was crying. Lance put his arms around her.

"The couple that adopted your baby were very fine people. They provided the best home ever for her. She couldn't have been more blessed. She is a happy, well adjusted little girl..."

"Then, I don't understand why I'm here," Sara said.

The lawyer handed her a letter. "This is to you from the adoptive parents."

She opened it and began to read. "Dear Sara, Let us first say thank you for giving us such a wonderful gift, our daughter. She has been a joy to us from the day we picked her up at the hospital. We would never have known the joy of being parents if not for your unselfish choice to give your baby to us. We know this was hard for you, cause we know how much you loved her; the nurse told us. Now, we want to do for you what you did for us; the precious little girl that you gave to us, we're giving her back to you. You see, Sara, if you are reading this letter then it means both of us are gone; we know that will probably never happen, but we're not taking any chances with our daughter's future. If we are no longer here to take care of our little girl, then we want her real mother to raise her. We named her Sara Brianna. We wanted her to always have a part of her mother with her, and when she was old enough to understand, we told her about you, and that you loved her. We call her Brie. We know that we can rest in peace knowing that our little girl will be safe in your love and care. We have one favor to ask of you. Brie has been raised in church and we ask that you will take her to church, so the strong values that she learns there, will always be a part of her life. Gratefully, Tim and Kari Horton."

Sara's hands were shaking as she finished reading the letter. "What does this mean?" she cried, tears blinding her eyes.

"Tim and Kari Horton were killed last week in a automobile accident on their way to work..."

"And, my baby, was she hurt?"

"No, they had already dropped her off at school."

102

Sara sobbed as she thought of the pain her daughter was going through, losing both of her parents like that. "Where is she?"

"Tim and Kari had no living relatives, so she's staying with friends..."

"Can I see her?" she blurted out, not grasping the reality of the situation.

"That depends on you and whether you're willing to take your daughter home with you and raise her; if not, then we feel it would be best for her not to see you."

Sara cried out, putting her hand over her mouth. "I can get my baby back. I can be her mother and have her with me for the rest of her life. Oh, yes, Mr. Owens, I want my little girl---with all my heart I want her."

"Are you willing to abide by the wishes of her parents and take her to church and make sure she has a strong Christian upbringing?"

"Yes, I go to church regularly and I will see to it that she goes too."

"Well, I guess all that is left is the financial arrangements," the lawyer said. "You will receive legal documents concerning this, but I'll brief it to you. Tim and Kari left everything to their daughter, of course, but they put it in a trust fund with you as the legal guardian, having the power of attorney. You will have access to the money in order to provide for the little girl in the fashion she is accustomed. The estate is sizable so there will be no money problems. Feel free to use the money for yourself as well as for your daughter. That's what they wanted."

"I am a designer and I make more than enough money for both my daughter and me. I want the money from her parents estate to be put in a fund for her college education, and also to do with as she pleases when she turns twenty one."

"Are you sure?" the lawyer asked with concern. "What if the time comes when you don't make enough money, then what? This is a big estate you're giving up. Maybe, you should think about it."

"No," she said. "Draw up the necessary papers and I'll sign them. Now, when do I get to see my daughter?"

"We didn't know how you would react to this, so the little girl is not here. Come back tomorrow and you can take her home with you."

"Thank you," she cried, wiping tears that ran down her face.

Sara couldn't stop crying as she sat in the car beside Lance.

"I'll never understand women," he commented. "You cry when you're sad and you cry when you're happy. I don't think you're sad, so those must be happy tears."

She nodded. "I'm so happy. I never thought I'd see my little girl again, now I'm going to take her home with me. She's going to be my daughter, our daughter. Just think, honey, tomorrow we're going to get our little girl."

Lance squirmed nervously, trying to find the right way to say what had to be said. "Sara, we need to talk about this," he said, cautiously. "Do you think it's a good idea to snatch the little girl out of the only place she's ever known and set her down in a strange place among strangers, without first giving her a chance to adjust to us?"

Sara looked at him with a surprised look in her eyes. "What are you suggesting, Lance?"

"I'm just saying maybe you should spend time with her first before actually taking her into your home. Get to know each other."

"And why would you suggest that, Lance?" she asked, a bit sharply. "Is it for her benefit, my benefit, or perhaps your benefit? Do you not want her to be a part of our family?"

Lance knew he was treading in dangerous waters, but he had to speak his mind. "Honey, I'll admit when I asked you to marry me, I thought it would be just you and

104

me for a couple of years or so before we started a family. I'm not sure I'm ready to take on the responsibility of raising a daughter right now. I don't think I'd even know where to start."

"Lance, you're making this hard for me," she said, tears running down her face. "You're forcing me to choose between my little girl and you; and there can only be one choice; I gave up my baby once, I won't do it again. I love you, Lance, but the wedding is off." She pulled the ring off her finger and handed it to him.

"Baby, don't do this," he pleaded. "We'll work it out. I'll get to know the little girl and I'm sure I'll learn to love her as much as you do. Just give me a little time. Let's go on with our plans. I don't want to lose you."

"No," she said, wiping away the tears, "I won't do that to my daughter. I won't bring her into a home where there is hostility against her. She's going to have a lot of things to adjust to. I won't put another one on her."

"So, that's the way it is, huh?" he said, with a twinge of anger. "You won't even consider my feelings..."

"Lance, if you could look down in my heart and see all the love imbedded there for my baby, then you wouldn't ask me to give her up, not even for one minute. If you really loved me, unselfishly, you wouldn't ask me anyway. That's the way love is."

"But, I do love you, Sara, with all my heart, and if it's selfish to want just you for awhile, then I am selfish, but that's me, honey, and I can't change who I am. I know in time I'd come to love your little girl, but if you're not willing to give me that time..."

"I'm not willing," she stated firmly. "I'm taking my daughter home tomorrow, so I guess we'll say our goodbyes tonight."

He pulled the car over to a roadside park and pulled her into his arms. "Oh, Sara, is there not someway we can work this out? I love you, baby, and the thought of not having you in my life scares me." He kissed her tenderly.

She responded to his kiss, then, shook her head. "Putting my daughter on hold, while you get to know her and learn to love her, is not an option. She's going home with me tomorrow and that's final, and since you can't accept that, there's no chance for us."

Lance never cried, but big tears were running down his cheeks now as he faced losing the woman who had won his heart; the woman he'd had been willing to give up his fast lifestyle, to marry. He offered the ring back to her. "Honey, please don't shut this door between us. Take the ring back and we'll put our wedding on hold until we have a chance to work this out, give the little girl and me a chance to get to know each other; to bond."

Sara wiped away more tears. "What if, after you go through this bonding period, you still can't love and accept her as your daughter, then what? How would I explain to my little girl that the man she thought was going to be her father, had changed his mind, and didn't want to be her father after all? Tell me Lance, how would I explain that to her?"

"Oh, Sara, hold me," he cried, "This is tearing my heart out. I love you so much, and I'm willing to try your terms; I'd do anything to keep from losing you; but I know that's not what's best for you and your daughter. You're right, Sara, you can't bring your little girl into a home where there is hostility; and I can't promise you that there wouldn't be a little hostility on my part, as least to begin with."

"I guess this is goodbye then," she said, her heart breaking inside her. She didn't love him any less because of how he felt; his feelings were a part of who he was, a part of the man she loved with all her heart, the man who would possess her heart forever. It hurt so much to give him up; but there would never be a choice when it came to him or her daughter. As much as she loved him, she would never forsake her little girl again.

They held on to each other, weeping together, trying to find a way to say goodbye. Lance knew it was his fault, and he wished with all his being that he could feel differently, but for now he couldn't.

The shadows of twilight were falling when Lance moved away from her and started the engine. "I'll get you settled safely in a hotel," he said, brushing the tears away and tenderly caressing her face, "then, I'm heading home. I'll call a taxi to take me to the airport and leave the rental car with you." He pulled out onto the street and drove until he found a hotel that was suitable for Sara to spend the night.

"What are your plans," he asked, as they stood in the lobby, after he had made the reservations. "Do you need a private jet to take you back to Nashville?"

The tears started again as Sara looked at this kind, wonderful man, so considerate and generous; always thinking of her. She wanted to throw herself in his arms and tell him they'd work it out somehow, but she couldn't; as long as he had these feelings, it could never work out for them.

She shook her head. "No, I'm going to rent a car and drive back to Nashville. I want this to be a special time for my daughter and me, a time of fun and getting to know each other."

"Will I ever see you again?" he asked over the lump in his throat. "May I call you when I'm in town on business?"

"Let's give it a little time and then we'll see," she said tearfully. She stepped into his arms and kissed him. "Oh, Lance, be happy. I love you too much to want you to go through life sad and alone."

"You, too, Sara." He kissed her and then turned, and bolted out of the hotel. He didn't look back; to do so would be too painful.

Sara arrived at the attorney's office the next morning full of hope and joy at the thought of seeing her baby again after all these years. She had cried all night over losing Lance, but she had to put him out of her mind, and concentrate on her daughter, and their life together.

The receptionist took her into the same room where she had waited yesterday with Lance. Her heart cried out in pain; it was almost as if she could see him sitting there beside her, holding her hand. She wiped the tears away, she had to be composed and at ease when she met her daughter.

A muffled cry escaped her lips when the little girl walked into the office, holding on to the lawyer's hand. She had Sara's blonde hair and also her clear blue eyes. Seeing her standing there was almost like looking in a mirror at herself when she was a kid, except that Brie had a healthy glow about her that Sara never had as a child; one could see that her parents had taken good care of her.

"I'll leave you two alone," the lawyer said, and walked out and shut the door.

They stood there speechless, mother and daughter, looking at each other.

Finally, the girl broke the silence. "Are you my real mother?"

"I'm your birth mother," Sara replied. "Kari Horton, the woman who loved you and took care of you all these years---she's your real mother."

"They said you loved me."

"I loved you more than anything on this earth," Sara cried. "The hardest thing I ever did was to give you up."

"Why did you? Mom and Dad never told me why you gave me to them."

"Baby, this may be hard for you to understand, but please listen carefully. My mother was a cruel, uncaring woman. All of my life she put me down. She told me I was ugly, didn't know how to do anything right, and that I would never amount to anything. She said it so often that I believed her, and when I was fifteen years old, I ended up on the streets. I looked for love and acceptance from anyone who would give them to me. I trusted the wrong people and ended up pregnant and alone. I was scared to death. I saw this ad about a home for unwed mothers, so I gave them a call; thank God, I did. The people there were loving and kind, and, they helped me to believe in myself, so much that by the time you were born, I knew that I could keep you and take good care of you, so that's what I was going to do..."

"But, you gave me away," the young girl blurted out.

"I know, honey, let me finish the story. After you were born, I was so full of plans for our future. The folks at the home would help me, and everything was all set for me to take you home and raise you myself; then my mother sent word that she was coming to the hospital, and that she would take the baby and raise it as her own, and I could go back to school and get on with my life. My world crumbled around me. I knew then I couldn't keep you. I loved you too much to let her do to you what she had done to me, so I let you go. Sweetheart, as I held you in my arms and said goodbye to you, my heart broke into a million pieces, and there's been an empty space in my heart from that day on. I never forgot what it felt like to hold you in my arms and kiss you..."

"Mommy," Brie cried, and ran into her mother's arms. "I've had an empty spot in my heart too, but I never knew why until now. I guess, somehow, I remembered those hugs and kisses you gave me that day, too."

Sara clung to her daughter and they wept in each other's arms. "Thank you God for giving me another chance with my baby," she prayed under her breath. Happiness filled her heart as she held her little girl close, and memories of the pain of losing Lance was replaced with joy; the wondrous joy of having her daughter back in her arms.

Lance walked into the office the next day, disheveled and weary. Belle took one look at him and gasped. She hurried over to him and put her arms around him.

"What happened, Lance," she asked anxiously. "Did Sara get bad news?"

"Not for her," he mumbled, almost incoherently. "It was wonderful news for Sara, but it cost us our future; the wedding is off."

"Lance, it can't be that bad," Belle said. "Tell me what happened."

"Sara got her little girl back, the baby she gave up all those years ago…"

"That's wonderful news," Belle exclaimed, "I'm sure Sara must be so happy." Then looking puzzled, she asked, "How could that make you call off the wedding?"

"Well, a, I wasn't as happy about it as she was."

"Lance, you didn't tell her that."

"Yeah, I'm afraid I did, and she gave me back my engagement ring and called off the wedding."

"Call her and tell her you've changed your mind. Please, Lance, make things right with her, before it goes any further."

He shook his head. "As much as it hurts to admit it, she's right, Belle. I couldn't give that little girl the love she needs from a father, not yet anyway. I was planning on it just being Sara and me for a couple of years before we started a family, and I'm not sure how I would react to the little girl being there; that could do a lot of damage to Sara's daughter. So, calling off the wedding was the right thing to do, even though it hurts like thunder."

"Well, I'm not giving up on you two, and I don't want you to, either. There's got to be a way, and I'm going to find it," she said, determinedly.

Chapter 14

"Chief Bristol has checked out the jails in your area, and he is sure that Cassie's mother is not being held in any of them," Kent told Andy when he called him to update him on what was happening with the case. "He's also checked out the nearby hospitals, and came up empty handed. He thinks they may be hiding her in a mental institution; is there one close to you?"

"Yeah, there's one on the outskirts of town," Andy answered. "But, I don't know much about it. Let me put Angelina on the line."

Kent explained the situation to her. "What do you know about the mental institution there?" he asked.

"Not much," she answered. "But, I can find out more. In a couple of weeks, as part of our school work, we're going to be visiting and working in the surrounding hospitals; I can volunteer to work there."

"I'm not sure the chief would want you to do that," Kent told her. "If she is there, you could be in danger."

"Has the chief got a better plan?"

"Probably not. I'll call and talk to him as soon as I hang up and I'll get back to you," Kent said, then talked a little more to Andy and hung up.

"Honey, I'm not sure I want you to do this," Andy said, concern in his voice. "I don't want you to risk your life. Let the experts take care of it, they've been trained in matters like this."

"I may be the only chance we've got to find Rebecca Bowman," she told him. "And, if that's the case, I can't let Cassie down. I don't think there will be a lot of danger in just finding out if she is there or not, since I'll have the perfect cover."

"Sweetheart, that may be well and true, but I still don't like it."

"We'll wait and see what Chief Bristol has to say," Angelina said.

The call from the chief came a couple of hours later. "Put your wife on the phone," he said when Andy answered.

"Mrs. Winslow, how much freedom will you have to look around for the Bowman woman, if you go in there?"

"I don't know," she replied. "I'd have to play it by ear. But, if she's there, I think I could find her without raising suspicions."

"I don't usually use civilians, but you may be the only choice we have. But, before I'll even consider letting you work undercover, I would want to be absolutely sure you are adequately protected at all times, and, I'll need a little time to get everything in place."

"Well, it will be about three weeks before we actually get started on this assignment. Will that give you enough time?"

"I think so, but first, I'll have to be able to get all of my people in place without a chance of anyone suspecting who they are. They will have to blend naturally into their surroundings," he said. "I'll get back to you, if and when, this is completed. Don't do anything until you hear from me."

"What did the chief say?" Andy asked, after they hung up.

"He said I might be the only chance they have to find out if Cassie's mother is in that sanitarian..."

"No," Andy interrupted. "I won't let you do it."

"He will have his people there working undercover," she explained. "I would be well protected."

Andy shook his head. "No, Angelina. There's got to be another way."

"Let's wait until we hear back from Chief Bristol, and then we can have this conversation, okay?"

"Okay," he said, taking her in his arms. He didn't think any amount of talking would convince him to allow his wife to be put in that kind of danger.

Roseanna's phone rang. "Hello," she said.

"Hon, this is Kent, and we need your help."

"Okay," she said. "What can I do?"

"We're sending a police artist out to talk to Cassie to see if they can come up with a sketch of the man who bought her, but no one can know why he's there, so that's where you come in. He will be posing as a reporter coming there to interview you; there will be another agent with him, posing as a photographer, to make things look on the up and up. These will be Chief Bristol's men..."

"Did I know them, before, in Nashville, when the drug bust went down?"

"No, I don't believe either of these men were in on that."

"When are they coming?"

"We'd like to send them out tomorrow if that's okay."

"Sure," she said. "Should I bring Cassie here to our house, or do you want me to go to Mama's?"

"I think your house would be better, since that's where an interview with you would normally take place," Kent said. "I'm almost certain that no one would ever connect her with any of you, but, we can't take a chance on it."

"Cassie and Isabelle have become best friends, so I'll have her to come over and spend the night."

"Good," he said. "We'll set it up for tomorrow then. The men's names are Brock and Mason, and they will show their badges. Just so you will recognize them, Brock is a little over six foot tall, and slim with black hair; Mason is shorter, with light brown hair, and he's a little bald."

113

"Okay, I'll be ready."

"Thanks, honey, I knew we could depend on you," Kent said. "Give your family our love and I'll be back in touch with you."

Roseanna called Mama and told her the plan. "Why don't you bring Cassie over as soon as Steve finishes with her lessons for today," she suggested. "She can spend the night with us and be here tomorrow when the FBI agents arrive. Isabelle will be thrilled to have her friend here to play with."

The agents arrived around ten the next morning. They showed the proper I.D., and Roseanna looked them over, making sure they fit the description that Kent had given her. Everything checked out, so she invited them in.

They got right down to business. The artist led Cassie through it by asking questions. He could see she was tense, so he tried to put her mind at ease.

"Don't be nervous, Cassie, just tell me what you remember about the man."

She shook her head. "I don't remember much---I was so scared."

"You may remember more than you think," Brock said. "How was he built, was he tall or short, slim or fat?"

Cassie let her mind go back to that horrible day. She tried to remember what the man looked like. "He wasn't as tall as you, but he was taller than the man that's with you. He wasn't fat, really, I guess you'd call him pudgy, and, his stomach hung down over his belt."

"Average height, a little on the fat side with a big belly," the artist mumbled as he started drawing a sketch of the man.

"Okay, Cassie, you're doing great, now try to feature his face and head. Was his face full or thin?"

Cassie visualized the scene when the man opened the door to let her in. She could see him standing there, looking her over, his jaws all puffed out as he grinned at her in that

114

creepy way. "His face was full," she answered. "He grinned at me in a way that made my skin crawl, and I noticed that his teeth were uneven; and he had thick bushy eyebrows." She started trembling as she relived the whole scene with that terrible man.

The agent reached out and took her hands. "We'll stop if this is too painful for you, Cassie," he said, compassionately. "But, if you can go on, the more we know about this man, the sooner we'll find him."

"What else do you want to know?"

"Was he clean shaven or did he have a beard?"

"He didn't have a beard."

"Did he wear glasses?"

"He didn't have any on while I was there."

"Okay, his eyes, were they close set or far apart? Was there anything special you noticed about them, the color maybe…"

"No," she answered quickly. "I don't know what color they are, but they were beady; squinty-like."

"Good, that could mean he usually wears glasses or at least needs to," the agent said, excitedly, as he continued to draw. "Okay, now, his hair. Did he have a full head of hair, or was he bald or getting bald?"

Cassie shut her eyes and tried to remember. She cringed as a picture of the man flashed through her mind, and she could feel his touch on her skin. "He had lots of hair, and it was dark, not real dark, but darker than blonde. It had streaks of gray running through it."

Brock drew a few more features on the paper, then, he showed it to Cassie. "Is this the man?"

"His nose was bigger, his eyes a little more squinty, and his hair wasn't quite that well groomed."

The man made some changes, then, showed the picture to Cassie, again.

She gasped. "That's him! That's the man!" Her breath came in deep gulps as she looked into the face of the man who had tried to hurt her.

The agent put his arms around her. "Don't worry, Cassie, that man will never touch you again. With the description you've given me, we should be able to track him down in no time. Now, I want you to talk to my partner and tell him all you remember about the man's house."

Mason had been taking pictures of Roseanna to make it seem realistic in case someone was watching. Now, Brock would interview her.

"Cassie, what do you remember seeing as you came into sight of the man's house?" Mason asked, getting ready to take notes.

"It was a big house and was pretty much hidden by lots of tall trees. We drove down a long driveway before we reached the house. There were no other houses in sight."

"Was the house brick or wood?"

"It was red brick with dark shutters."

"The inside of the house, do you remember anything at all about it?"

"It was dark; the blinds in the front room were all drawn," she said, trying to remember more about the house. "Oh yes, the bathroom didn't have a window or a lock on the door. That's all I remember. I didn't notice the name of the street."

"You've done great, Cassie." Mason said. "Andy Winslow told us the name of the street where he found you, so it shouldn't be too difficult to find the man's house. Thank you so very much, and, if you ever decide to go into law enforcement, the FBI could sure use someone with your ability to observe things around you."

After the men left, Roseanna put her arms around Cassie. "Honey, I am so proud of you. You're a brave little girl, and, I feel certain that with all the information you

116

were able to give them, they'll have that man behind bars in no time."

Andy was still brooding over the situation when Chief Bristol called back later that week. "I don't want my wife doing this," he said.

"Of course, it will up to you and your wife to make the final decision," Chief Bristol told him. "But, I'd like to explain the plans we've made to the two of you. Can you put her on the phone, too?"

"Yes," Andy replied, and called Angelina. "Pick up the phone in the bedroom, honey. It's Chief Bristol."

The chief went over his plans to put his people in key positions at the hospital. "Angelina will never be out of their sight," he assured them. "My people will be ready to step in at a moment's notice if it comes to that."

"How will I know your people?" she asked.

"You won't," the chief answered. "That way there will be no knowing looks or nods in their direction. Even though you don't know them, they will all know you and keep you under close surveillance at all times. You won't make a move that they don't know about."

"Okay, I'm convinced," she said. "Just tell me what to do."

"Just a minute," Andy spoke up. "I know you think you have all the bases covered, but what if there's a slip-up, what happens to Angelina then?"

"These people are pros, they will do their job to perfection," Chief Bristol said. "I can assure you there won't be a slip-up."

"Andy, I want to do this," Angelina said. "If she is there I'm probably the only one that find her, and get her out safely. Honey, please don't fight me on this. I've got to do all that I can to help find Cassie's mother. I promised her."

"Okay," he said, "but, if anything happens to you..."

117

Chapter 15

Jesse was walking out of the office on Friday afternoon when the phone rang. Debbie had left for the day, so he answered it.

"Counseling Clinic."

"Mr. J. Michael Lawrence, please."

"This is he. How may I help you?"

"Mr. Lawrence, I'm a medic in New Orleans, and we just picked up one of your patients who took an overdose of sleeping pills. Your card was on the table."

"Who is it?" Jesse asked, concerned that one of his patients would try to commit suicide.

"Her name is Pamela Connors."

Jesse grimaced. "Is she going to make it?"

"I think she will pull through this time, but, from the emotional condition she's in, if she doesn't get help, I believe she will try it again. That's why I called you."

Jesse faltered a moment, reflecting on what this could do to his family. But he had to go; his code of ethics wouldn't let him refuse to help any of his patients; not even Pamela.

"I'll be there as soon as possible," he said and hung up the phone.

"Belle," he whispered, wondering how she would react to this. It had been less than a week since they'd gone to Pamela's to break the news to her about the house. He thought of the big fight they'd had afterward concerning the money he'd spent on Pamela's ring. Belle was still upset that he wouldn't tell her where he got the money to pay for the ring, but at least she was talking to him again; now this. "I need Belle there with me, so I'd better not tell her up front

118

what's going on," he muttered to himself. "I'll explain it to her later."

He dialed his home number. "Sweetheart, throw some things into a suitcase, you and I are going to New Orleans for the weekend."

He dialed a hotel in New Orleans and made reservations.

In a short time they were on their way.

"Jesse, you're the most romantic man in the world," Belle said, snuggling close to him. "This is like a second honeymoon, just you and me, spending the whole weekend in New Orleans. Thanks, honey for planning this wonderful surprise."

"I'm dead," Jesse mumbled under his breath and wished he had told her the truth about the trip. He had to tell her now.

"Belle, sweetheart, this is not exactly a pleasure trip," he explained. "We will have lots of time to spend with each other, but I was called to New Orleans by a medic. A patient of mine took an overdose of sleeping pills, and my card was on the table. I'm sorry, baby, I should have told you."

A look of disappointment covered Belle's face. "Why didn't you, Jesse?"

"I need you there with me, Belle, and I didn't know if you'd come if you knew the truth," he said, nervously. He hesitated a moment. "Honey, the patient is Pamela."

She scooted as far away from him as she could, a look of anger and hurt filling her eyes.

He reached over and took her hand. "Sweetheart, do you think I wanted to come? I have an obligation to all of my patients, even Pamela, and whether I like it or not, I've got to try to help her, to make sure she doesn't do this again."

Belle snatched her hand out of his and sat there in hostile silence.

"I think this is a mistake," Jesse said. "My main concern is, and always will be you, Belle, so I'm going to call a friend of mine in New Orleans, and get him to take over the case. He's a very good counselor, and..."

"No," Belle broke in. "You can't do that, Jesse. As much as I loathe Pamela, I don't want to see her kill herself, and she probably won't listen to anyone but you. So, no matter how much it hurts, you have to do this."

"Are you sure honey?"

She nodded, knowing there was no other choice.

"Thanks, sweetheart," he said. "I called ahead and reserved a room in a hotel near the hospital, so I'll drop you off there."

"No, I'll go to the hospital with you and stay in the waiting room in case you need me."

Jesse smiled gratefully. Belle was the most understanding woman in the world and he was lucky to have her for his wife.

A little while later, Jesse walked into Pamela's room. He pulled a chair close to the bed and sat down. He took her hand. "Pamela," he said, in a soft gentle tone.

Pamela stirred and opened her eyes. "Jesse," she mumbled feebly, her mouth feeling like it was full of cotton. "How?"

"They found my card in your room and called me."

"And you came?"

"Of course I came..."

"But why?"

"Pamela, you tried to kill yourself. I'm your counselor and I care about what happens to you," he said. "Now tell me why you did this?"

She turned her head away.

"If you don't talk to me and tell me why you took those sleeping pills, then I can't help you."

"I can't," she muttered and started crying.

120

Belle got restless in the waiting room and walked to Pamela's room. The door was ajar, so she listened, even though she knew she shouldn't. She watched as Jesse reached out and took Pamela's other hand.

"Pamela, please let me help you..."

"Jesse, what we had wasn't all bad, was it?" she asked, as if she didn't hear him. "When you made those commitments to me, you did care for me, didn't you?"

He had to be careful how he answered her. She was fragile. The least little thing could send her over the edge. "Of course I cared for you, and it wasn't all bad, there were good times."

Belle wanted to walk away but her feet wouldn't budge.

"Pamela, you need to tell me why you tried to kill yourself when you have so much to live for. You're a successful lawyer, you're beautiful, and you have all the money you could ever want; these are the things that are important to you."

"Not anymore," she said and started crying again. "Jesse, I don't want to live."

"But why?" he asked again. "I don't understand."

"Jesse, the night I came to your house, you asked me if I was pregnant and I said no; I lied..."

"You're going to have a baby?"

Belle gasped and ran down the corridor and out the main door.

"The sleeping pills---did they hurt the baby?" Jesse asked, afraid to hear the answer. "Pamela, what about the baby?"

Tears filled her eyes. "Jesse, I tried everyway I knew to get you to come back to me, short of telling you about the baby; and, I had hopes that I would get you back, one way or another, until the other night when you told me your plans concerning the house. I knew then it was all over

121

between us and I got afraid. I didn't know how to be a mother, and I didn't want to raise the baby by myself..."

"So, you swallowed a bottle of sleeping pills to get rid of the baby," he said, angrily.

"No, it wasn't like that," she said, clutching at his arm. "I'm sorry, Jesse, please, forgive me. The day after you came to my house, I did a terrible thing. I had an abortion."

"You didn't!" he stormed, forgetting momentarily how fragile she was. "You had no right to do that to our child. What kind of woman are you, killing your own baby like that?"

She was sobbing hysterically now. "I thought I was the kind of woman who could get rid of the baby without a second thought, but I was wrong, Jesse. I walked out of that clinic, feeling dead and empty inside, and I haven't had a moments peace since; that's why I took the sleeping pills. I wanted die. Oh Jesse, I don't want my baby to be dead. I want him back. I want to hold him in my arms and be his mother."

Jesse pulled her into his arms and held her compassionately. He was very angry with her and he would deal with that later---now she needed him to hold her.

Blinded by tears, Belle ran down the street toward the hotel. Pamela was having Jesse's baby---what would that do to them---to Mikey and Annie? "Oh, God," she cried, "How can we get through this?"

She wiped her tears and tried to compose herself as she walked into the lobby of the hotel. "I'm Mrs. Jesse Lawrence, and we have a reservation," she told the man behind the desk.

"Yes, Mrs. Lawrence," the man said, handing her the key, with a worried look on his face. "Did I do the right thing?" he pondered aloud, as Belle got into the elevator.

Belle stepped off the elevator, unlocked the door and walked in. "Wow!" she exclaimed, her eyes wide with wonder. "A whole suite---it's so romantic. Jesse planned a special weekend for us after all. He wanted to surprise me." She sighed happily, walking around the suite, admiring its beauty. Fresh cut flowers in charming vases were scattered around, candles were everywhere, and soft music was playing. "A Jacuzzi," she said, excitedly, as she finished her tour of the rooms. "Wow, he must have paid a fortune for this." She felt so special, like a princess, in a beautiful palace. "I'm really special to Jesse," she said, feeling a twinge of guilt for being so upset with him earlier. She'd let him know it was okay about the baby, that, they would work it out somehow. "I've got to do something special for him," she muttered, and her wifely instincts took over. Jesse had not eaten supper before they left home so he would be starved when he got to the hotel. "I'll call room service and order his favorite meal." She picked up the phone and ordered a big juicy steak, and baked potato. "Make the steak medium well and bring lots of butter."

"Will do," the voice on the other end of the line said.

A little while later a knock and a voice yelling, "Room Service" let Belle know the meal was here. She opened the door and let the young man in.

"You sure changed your order from the usual one I bring to you and Mr. Lawrence in this suite," he remarked, as he sat the tray down on the table.

Belle raised her eyebrows in surprise. "What do you mean?"

"You know, you and Mr. Lawrence usually order caviar, cheese and crackers, strawberries in cream, a bottle of fine wine, and several bottles of hard liquor. You never order a meal like this. It must be a special occasion."

"You might say that," Belle replied, wanting to find out more about Jesse and this suite.

"If you don't mind me saying so," the young man said, "I think you're much prettier as a brunette, than you were as a blonde. Even in this dim candle light I can see that brown hair suits you better."

"Thank you," Belle said, with a lump in her throat as reality hit her. Jesse had been here before with Pamela. "How dare he bring me here," she fumed to herself as she plotted a plan to get even with him. "Mr. Lawrence loves A-1 sauce on his steaks, if you don't mind bringing some up, and also bring some Louisiana Hot Sauce and cayenne pepper. He likes his food hot and spicy, and I have a special way of mixing them, to satisfy his taste buds."

The young man came back in a few minutes with the items that Belle had ordered. "Thank you so much," she said, tipping him generously. She knew he would lose his job if the management found out that he had talked to her about the things that went on in this room, even though he thought he was talking to Pamela. She couldn't believe he had mistaken her for that woman. "I won't tell Jesse how I found out," she purposed, and went to work mixing the special sauce for him.

Jesse called a few minutes later. He had gone looking for her in the waiting room and when she wasn't there, he called her on her cell phone. "I'm finished here," he said. "Meet me in the lobby and we can go to the hotel."

"I'm already at the hotel," she said sweetly, "just waiting for my husband to get here. I walked, so the car is still in the hospital parking lot."

"Belle, you didn't," he scolded. "You shouldn't be walking the streets alone at night. It's not safe."

"I made it fine," she said, "so stop fretting."

Jesse parked the car in the parking garage of the hotel and hurried inside. He had forgotten to get the room number from Belle, so he stopped at the front desk. "How's it going, Charlie?" he asked pleasantly.

"Okay, I hope sir," he answered, handing Jesse the key to the suite.

Jesse turned pale when he saw that it was the key to the suite he'd shared with Pamela. "We can't stay there," he said, "give us another room."

"There are no more rooms," the man informed him. "In fact, there are no rooms anywhere for miles around because of the big festival that's going on."

"What am I going to do?" Jesse moaned. "I can't stay there with Belle..."

"She'd never know," the man pointed out.

"But I know, and I'd never do that to Belle; she's too precious to me," Jesse told the man. "I'll have to find a way to explain it to her."

"I'm sorry, Mr. Lawrence, you've always wanted that room before, so when you called for reservations, I just assumed..."

"It's not your fault," Jesse said. "I should have made myself clear." He walked dejectedly toward the elevator. He stood before the door of the suite, hesitantly; but he had to go in sooner or later, so he unlocked the door.

Belle met him with a kiss. "I knew you'd be starved, so I ordered room service, and it's ready and waiting for you."

Jesse lifted the lid from the container. "Steak," he exclaimed. "Belle, I don't deserve all this loving care you're giving me."

"Sweetheart, you deserve everything you're getting from me, and more." She watched as he picked up the bottle of A-1 sauce and poured it lavishly over his steak.

He took a big bite and gasped for breath. He jumped up and ran to the sink and filled a glass with water. He swigged it down in big gulps. He filled it again and again. "What happened?" he finally gasped, his mouth and throat burning like they were on fire.

"You're used to things being hot and spicy in this room, and I didn't want to disappoint you, so I fixed up a special sauce for you using hot sauce and cayenne pepper."

"Why, Belle?" he asked with a hurt look in his eye that far outweighed the pain in his mouth and throat. How could Belle do this to him?

"I wanted to hurt you the way you hurt me," she replied angrily. "When I walked in here and saw this cozy, romantic suite, I was overjoyed. I felt so loved and special, like a beautiful princess in a fairy tale. I knew I was important to you, for you to have planned this romantic weekend, just for me. Then, I found out the truth." Tears were rolling down her face. "How could you, Jesse Lawrence, how could you bring me here to your special little love nest?"

She knew, but how? "I'd never do that to you, Belle. It was a mistake. I didn't reserve this suite for us."

"Of course not," she said, "You'd never reserve a special place like this for me; I'm just your wife. Places like this are for Pamela..."

"Belle, honey..."

"Don't you honey me, Jesse Lawrence!" she screamed. "I've worked my fingers to the bone for you; I cleaned your house, I cooked your meals, I scrubbed your toilet, I bore your kids---do you know how painful it is to have a baby? Well, I hope Pamela feels every pain I did, only double, when she has that brat of yours!"

She grabbed her hairdryer and hurled it at Jesse. He ducked, but not in time. It hit him on the side of the face. "What did all of that hard work and pain get me---nothing!" she screamed again. "You never did anything special for me! I wasn't important enough for things like this. You saved all the special things for Pamela; that big diamond ring, this romantic little hide away, while all I ever got from you was hard work and heartache!" She picked up a table lamp and started to throw it at him, but he grabbed her and took it from her.

126

"Let go of me," she screamed, kicking him on the shin with all her might. "I'm getting out of here. I'm going home."

"You're not going anywhere tonight," he told her firmly. "It's not safe for you to be out on the highway this time of night, and since every hotel for miles around is booked solid, you're going to stay right here."

"No, I won't!" she yelled furiously. "I'd sleep on a slab of ice out in a freezing blizzard before I'd sleep in this place."

"Belle, we've got to talk," he said. "I can't stand what this is doing to you; you're at the breaking point, and it's all my fault. Every time we think we've got this all behind us; you find out something else about Pamela that hurts you, and I won't let that happen again." He took her hand. "Come sit on the couch beside me," he said, in a raspy voice. "I'm going to tell you everything that went on between Pamela and me; that way there'll be no more surprises."

"No," she yelled. "I'm not staying here…"

"Yes, you are. We're going to work this out tonight; now sit."

She could tell by the tone of his voice that he meant it, so she sat down.

He put his arms around her and held her close. She pushed him away. "Belle, please let me hold you. I don't think I can get the courage to tell you the things I need to, if I'm not holding on to you," he said. "I should have told you all this up front, but, I didn't want to hurt you more than I already had; these things were in the past, and I hoped you would never have to know about them; but it seems like the past always comes back to haunt us, so I'm going to tell you before you find out some other way; and honey, please listen to all of it, before you pass judgment on me."

She moved reluctantly back into his arms. "I won't promise you anything, but I will listen to what you've got to say."

"Belle, what I'm about to tell you is going to hurt you more than anything has ever hurt you. I just hope it doesn't shatter your faith in me. Honey, I haven't been completely honest with you. I let you think this thing between Pamela and me started the night you saw us at that Inn, but it actually started a few weeks before that. You remember the first Sunday we missed church and I went to the office; Pamela saw my van there and stopped by. She told me that she wanted me, then, she kissed me. Brad knocked on the door just then, and she left. I had no intention of taking her up on her offer. But she kept calling and coming by the office, and eventually we started taking long lunch breaks and going for walks in the park, picnics by the lake, and after work we'd go for long drives in the country. Flirting with her and sneaking around was fun and exciting; and, I was so angry with you, I guess I thought I had the right to get even. But, at that point, that's all it was Belle, just a flirtation. Then, one night we parked and things got out of hand; we kissed and would have gone farther, but I pulled away, and we didn't. It scared me that I had almost broken my marriage vows, and I was determined to break it off, but she insisted that we go to that Inn and talk things out. You know what happened then."

"When you were still living at home you were seeing her---all those nights, when I thought you were working late, you were with her? Those lonely nights I waited up hoping to work things out between us, you were out having fun with Pamela?" A tear slid down her face. "Please, Jesse, don't say anymore."

"I've got to, honey. You've got to hear everything," he said, taking a deep breath. "The other night I refused to tell you where I got the money to pay for Pamela's ring because I knew how much it would hurt you, but I'm going

128

to tell you now. Please, Belle, promise that you won't hate me."

"Spit it out, Jesse," she said angrily. "Did you buy the ring on credit---will we be paying for that big diamond the rest of our lives?"

"No, I paid cash for the ring." A tear rolled down his face. He'd rather die than to hurt Belle this way, but he had to tell her the truth. "Honey, I took the money from our savings account to pay for it…"

"Jesse, how could you," she gasped. "That was our money for emergences and the kids college fund. How could you spend our money on her?"

"I have no excuse," he said. "Since the bank statements came to my office, I intended to put the money back so you would never have to know, but I couldn't. Belle, I can't undo this, all I can do is to beg for your forgiveness. I have made some investments that will assure the kid's college fund, but, as for our money, it's gone, and, I can never make it right. Please forgive me, Belle."

"Forgive you, Jesse?" she cried. "You took our money, the money we'd scrimped years to save, and spent it on her; she ended up with a diamond ring worth thousands of dollars, and I ended up with nothing; I'm supposed to forgive you for that."

"At least hear me out, Belle," he pleaded, "our future depends on it."

She nodded, reluctantly. At this point she didn't believe he could say anything that would change her mind.

"As you know, I moved in with Pamela the day of the divorce hearing, and soon after that, we moved into the mansion, and life took a turn for the worse. Pamela threw a wild party for some of our married friends, and a few singles. It lasted the entire weekend and progressed from bad to worse. I was appalled by some of the things that went on there. God, help me, Belle, I went along with most of it; but when it was time to retire for the night; couples chose partners to sleep with, and they didn't choose their own husband or wife." A tear slid down his face.

"The first night I slept on the couch alone. But the next night I was so drunk I ended up with another man's wife, and the next morning when I woke up beside her, I got so sick, I threw up." More tears followed the first down his face. "When I let the devil get a foothold in my life, he dragged me all the way down to the bottom. My heart had lost the goodness that used to be there, now it was filled with lust. But, things had gone too far, even for my lustful heart, and I told Pamela that I would never again be a part of those parties. She said, 'Okay, Jesse, if that's the way you want it,' and, she never had another wild party. Pamela was used to that kind of life, and I felt like I owed her because she gave it up to please me, so we started having our own special weekends. We flew to places like Vegas, New York City, San Francisco and Mexico. One weekend we came to New Orleans, that's when we found this place, and it became our special place, our very own little love nest. It was fun and exciting, but deep down I hated myself. We spent most of our weekends here after that; that's why when I called for a room, they automatically gave me this suite."

"Jesse, don't," she pleaded. "I don't want to hear about your special times with that woman."

"Honey, I'm not telling you this to hurt you, but, to show you how very special you are to me."

"This is supposed to make me feel special?"

"Please, listen to the rest of it," he pleaded. "Pamela and I needed all those trinkets and special places because we had nothing else. We didn't have the things that you and I have; those weekends were all we had going for us." He paused. "Belle, every night that I spent with her, I'd lie there beside her, after she went to sleep, and think about you. My arms would ache to hold you, and I wished with all my heart that you were the one lying there beside me. I yearned for the goodness of you, your pure love that you gave so freely. Tears would soak my pillow as I remembered the wonderful life that I had thrown away. I hated what I was doing, but I felt like I was in a deep pit and couldn't climb out. I think I would have stayed there forever if not for you. Remember the day you brought the kids by the office to see me?"

She nodded.

"I had hit bottom and resigned myself to the fact that I was a part of that world, and that's all life would ever be for me; then the door to my private office opened and you walked in. Belle, remember the things we did that day; taking the kids to Ed's Drive-In for supper, buying the Christmas tree and decorating it, eating cookies that you had made. Just ordinary things, but to me they were so special. Honey, just spending that time with you and the kids gave me hope that life could be good again. Then, you invited me to spend Christmas with you. Belle, you'll never know how much that meant to me; it made me want to fight to get out of that pit, and become the kind of man you could be proud of again. And, the day you kidnapped me from Pamela's; I saw how much you cared, and it gave me the courage to try. It took a lot of help from God, but I made it. I cried out to Him, and He pulled me up out of all that lust; cleansed me and made my heart pure again."

"I'm glad, Jesse, but what has that got to do with me?"

"What I'm trying to say, honey, is that when I'm with you I don't need all those special places and things to make me happy. Just doing ordinary things like sitting across the dinner table from you, romping in the den with the kids, or, relaxing after supper, watching TV together, or just lying in bed talking for hours; it doesn't matter where we are or what we're doing, it's special to me, because, I'm doing them with you. Belle, you are all my special times and

131

places. I don't need all those trinkets to keep me happy and content. I only need you."

She started crying. "Jesse, I understand what you're saying, and I wish I could say it makes everything right between us, but it doesn't. I know you love me. I can see it in your eyes every time you look at me. I can feel it in your touch, and you show it by the way you work so hard to take care of the kids and me. But knowing that doesn't stop the hurting."

He pulled her closer. "Belle, I'm sorry. I thought telling you all this would help you see just how special you are to me, but it's only hurt you more. Please forgive me." A tear ran down his face. "Honey, I wish there was some way I could stop the hurting, and help you to believe in me again."

"I know you're a good man, and I love you with all my heart. I do believe in you, but the things I'd heard and found out this past week have hurt me deeply." She trembled as unquenchable tears ran down her face. "Jesse," she cried, "you loved Pamela; you were going to marry her. You bought her that ring...she was special to you."

"Honey," he said, taking her in his arms. "I guess I did love Pamela in some perverted way, and yes, we had our special times together, but she was never special to me. Belle, you're the only woman who could ever be special to me. I know how much I've hurt you, and I don't deserve your love. My sweet Belle..." His voice broke as tears ran down his face. "I love you with all my heart, but I know you can't deal with all of this right now, so I'll move into the guest room, unless you want me to move out of the house..."

"No, Jesse, I don't want you to move out," she cried. "I've forgiven you and I do love you, but there's these feelings of resentment against you for all the special times you shared with Pamela; the two of you having fun together, all the money you spent to make her happy. The fact that you were planning to marry her and she was going to take

132

my place in your life hurts me deep inside. I don't know how to handle this hurt; and, I need you to stay home and help me work through all of it, that is, if you're sure you don't mind moving into the guest room until I can resolve these feelings."

"I'm sure Belle. Honey, I'd do anything to take this hurt away from you," he said, "but I believe it is imbedded so deep inside you, that only an inner healing from God can erase it completely. It has probably been building up ever since this mess first started, and hurt has piled up on top of hurt, until there is so much that you can't handle it. Honey, we need to pray right now."

"Here, in this room?" she blurted out.

"What better place to pray then on the devils turf? Belle, he used this place against me, to try to keep me in his clutches; now, we can use it against him, to put him in his place."

She nodded, and fell to her knees. Jesse knelt beside her and took her in his arms and they prayed, there on the devils territory, for the healing process to start.

Later, Jesse sat on the couch and held her until the tears stopped and she fell asleep in his arms. He didn't want to wake her; and, since there were no memories in this suite that bothered him, and none that were important to him, they would stay here tonight. He needed to tell her about the abortion, and ask her how she found out about the baby; but that could wait 'til tomorrow; right now she needed to sleep, and he needed to hold her.

Chapter 16

"Brad, would you watch the boys later today? I want to go to New Orleans and shop for my outfit for the concert, and I want to take Isabelle and Cassie and get new outfits for them too." Roseanna had a concert scheduled in Nashville the middle part of June, and Isabelle was going to sing a song during the concert.

"Sure, sweetheart, but if you wait to leave after Isabelle gets out of school, won't that make you late getting home?"

"Yeah, will that be a problem?" Roseanna asked, thinking he might have an appointment.

"Not a problem, exactly, but I don't want the three of you out on the highway, alone, that time of night." Brad said. "Tell you what, I'll call mama and see if she can watch the boys, and I'll go with you."

"Honey, we might shop for hours and you'll be so bored."

"I'd rather be bored than for the three of you to be in danger," he said. "Don't worry about me, sweetheart, I'll be fine."

They picked Isabelle up from school that afternoon and got on their way. The two girls sat in the back seat, laughing and giggling, the way girls do.

"Brad, do you sense that there is something wrong between Belle and Jesse?" Roseanna asked quietly, so the girls wouldn't overhear. "They've been acting differently since they got back from New Orleans."

"Worried about your sister?" Brad asked, putting his arm around Roseanna and pulling her close. He leaned over and gave her a quick kiss.

She nodded and laid her head on his shoulder.

Isabelle shook her head when she saw the kiss. "Daddy kisses mommy a lot," she told Cassie, "even in the car."

"I never saw my daddy kiss my mama," Cassie said.

"I guess it's better for mommies and daddies to kiss a lot, then not to kiss at all," Isabelle surmised, thoughtfully, and dismissed it from her mind.

"Honey," Roseanna asked, "did Jesse explain to you why his face had that big bruise on it?"

"No, and he seemed to have trouble swallowing," Brad answered. "Belle didn't mention it to you?"

"Not a word, and that's not like her. Brad, do you think they had a fight?"

"If they did, it looks like Belle won the battle."

"Belle would never hurt Jesse," Roseanna said. "She's too sweet and gentle."

"Not always," Brad said, thinking back to a day years ago. "The day she drove my car into the bayou, with the two of us in it, she wasn't so sweet and gentle then."

"I'll check Belle out, and you can work on Jesse; surely one of us can find out what happened."

"Maybe, we should stay out of it, sweetheart," he suggested. "This may be something they need to work out between the two of them."

She nodded, but she knew she wouldn't leave it alone; one way or another, she would find out what happened.

"You girls can look around, but stay where either daddy or I can see you," Roseanna told Isabelle, as they went into one of the most exclusive shops in the mall. "We'll go to your department as soon as I'm finished here."

"I'll keep my eye on them," Brad promised. "You concentrate on shopping." They would get home much sooner if she didn't have to worry about the girls.

Isabelle and Cassie rummaged through rows of fancy gowns, holding different ones up to them, looking in the mirror, and giggling.

Cassie held a vibrant blue one up to her, and twirled and turned.

"Oh, that's you, dar-ling," Isabelle said, with the air of a grand lady. "It looks positively breathtaking on you." They doubled over giggling.

Brad noticed a saleslady looking at them with less than a friendly glare. "They're with me," he told her.

"Then, you should watch them more closely, sir," she said tartly.

"I apologize," he said, and motioned for the girls.

"We're just having fun, Daddy," Isabelle said.

"I know, sweetheart, but this nice lady doesn't want you having fun in her store." They walked over to a settee close by and sat down. "I hope your mama doesn't find anything she likes," he whispered. "I'd sure hate to spend money in this place."

Roseanna walked over, kissed Brad and put her arms around Isabelle and Cassie.

The saleslady who had been giving the girls the evil eye turned pale when she recognized Roseanna, and realized that she had just insulted the superstar's family. She hurried over to her. "Did ma-dam find everything satisfactorily?"

"Everything was fine," Roseanna replied. "I didn't find what I needed, so I'll check back later." Then she turned to the girls. "Let's see if we can find something for the two of you."

"Honey," Brad whispered, "can we go to another store to look for the girls clothes? I don't like this one."

136

"Okay, sweetheart, I'm sure you'll explain later," she said, then, with a thank you to the lady, they walked out of the store.

Roseanna's eyes flashed with anger when she heard the story. "You girls shouldn't have been playing with the merchandise, that's true, but I don't like the way that woman treated the three of you, so I'll shop elsewhere from now on."

They went to lots of stores in the mall and by the time they were finished shopping, Isabelle and Cassie were loaded down with packages filled with jeans and tops, dresses and shoes, and each had a purse of their choice, as well as some jewelry. Roseanna didn't have a single package.

"I guess I'm just so spoiled to Mavis' designs that nothing else pleases me," she sighed. "I'll give her a call and tell her what I want. Maybe, she can come up with something for Isabelle that goes with the outfit she designs for me."

"How about we eat now?" Brad suggested, "I'm two hours past the hungry stage."

"Sorry, honey," Roseanna told him. "I think we're all ready to eat."

"Where to?" he asked.

"Let's go to that nice restaurant out on the highway, where we can get adult food and the kids can get whatever they want."

"Sounds good to me," Brad said.

A couple of days later the phone rang. Roseanna answered.

"Hon, I think we may have a problem," Kent said, with concern in his voice.

"What's wrong, Kent?"

"You went shopping with the girls a couple of days ago, right?"

"Yeah, but how did you know?" She hadn't called Mavis about the clothes for the concert, so how would Kent know?

"Your picture made the Nashville papers, and, I'm afraid it will go nationwide," he explained. "The article said you were shopping with your daughter and her friend, and the photographer got a really clear picture of Cassie. Honey, if those people who are looking for her see that picture they will recognize her immediately."

"Oh, no," Roseanna cried. "I shouldn't have taken her out in public. I wasn't thinking. I can usually go places here without any fanfare. I don't even know when the photographer took the picture. I've put Cassie in danger."

"Honey, not only Cassie, but, all of you will be in danger if they see the picture, and figure out that she is there with you. It won't be too hard finding out where you live, as well known as you are," Kent said. "We've got to find a way to protect all of you, but that might be difficult. If we send officers in there, it will draw even more attention…"

"There are plenty of men here on the bayou," she said. "Men that know how to use guns, and we can trust all of them."

"Are you sure they are capable of protecting you? Could they shoot to kill if they had to?"

"They are hunters from way back and they are not afraid to use guns…"

"Hon, it's different shooting wild game, and shooting another human being. Could they do it?"

"They might not shoot to kill, but they'd sure know where to shoot, to put them out of commission; and there is not one man here that wouldn't do that, if it came down to our lives or theirs."

"Good," he said, "now let me talk to Brad and we'll make plans to make sure all of you stay safe."

Brad got on the phone and he and Kent laid out a strategy so that the LeBlanc house, and their house would always have two men there, with at least one of them having a gun.

"Be careful, Brad," Kent warned, "and be especially on your guard if a stranger shows up."

The stranger showed up three days later. He caught them off guard. Brad was sitting in his recliner, going over his sermon for Sunday morning, and Earl was napping on the couch. When the doorbell rang, Roseanna opened the door.

"Are you Roseanna, the singer?"

Before she could answer, Brad jumped up, rushed over and grabbed the man, holding his hands behind his back. "Get inside, sweetheart," he told Roseanna, as Earl ran to the door, holding a shotgun in his hands.

"Don't make a move, mister," Earl threatened, "or it'll be your last one."

"Please, I don't want any trouble," the man said, "I saw the picture in the paper, and I'm here about the girl..."

Earl shoved the shotgun right in the man's face.

"Surely you're not going to shoot me for that," he said, panic-stricken.

"That depends," Earl replied.

"What about the girl?" Brad asked, eying the man closely. He was tall and well built, probably in his late fifties, and had an honest look about him. All criminals *look* honest he reminded himself and tightened his grip on him.

"I think I may be her grandfather."

"When's the last time you saw your granddaughter?" Brad asked, knowing that Cassie had never seen her grandfather.

"I've never seen her," he replied, "but the little girl in the picture looks like my daughter, Rebecca, when she was a girl. The resemblance is so striking that I had to come and check it out."

139

He could still be lying, Brad thought to himself. "Why should I believe you?" he asked. "Anyone could get that information."

"Well, I have no way of proving that I am telling the truth, but, I can prove who I am," the man said. "I am Franklin Cassidy and my drivers license is in my wallet. It's in my left pocket."

Brad slowly took the wallet out and removed the driver's license. "Well, it appears you are Franklin Cassidy, but that still doesn't prove anything. Honey, call your father and tell him to bring Cassie over here right now."

"Cassie," the man repeated the name with a slight smile. "Her mother named her Cassie, after me. That should prove something."

"Not necessarily," Brad told him. "We'll wait 'til she gets here and see if she can identify you."

Ellis arrived with Cassie a few minutes later. "What's this all about," he asked. "Roseanna told me to get Cassie and my gun and hurry over here. What's going on?"

"We'll see in a minute," Brad answered. "Cassie, do you know this man? Have you ever seen a picture of him?"

"No sir, I've never seen him before, or a picture of him."

"Have you ever seen a picture of your grandfather? Do you know what he looks like?"

She shook her head. "Mama said grandmother burned all his pictures after he left, so I never saw a picture of him."

"Is there anyway that you would know if this man is your grandfather?"

"Are you my Grandfather Cassidy?" she asked.

"That's what we're trying to find out," Brad told her.

She looked at the man standing there. "Do you remember the story you used to tell my mother when she was small...?"

"About the wonderful little Baby, with lots of power and a love so big that He would help anyone who needed him?"

"Grandfather," she cried, and ran into his arms.

"Back away from him, Cassie," Ellis LeBlanc said. "We're still not sure…"

"I'm almost convinced," Brad said. He looked over at Franklin Cassidy. "I'm going to give you the benefit of the doubt, but we will all be watching you. You can stay here and visit with Cassie, but if we even get an inkling that you're out to harm her, we won't hesitate to shoot you."

He sat down on the couch and pulled Cassie onto his lap. "You look just like your mother," he said, wiping a tear away.

"Grandfather, why did you go off and leave mama? She loved you so much."

"Honey, leaving your mother was the hardest thing I ever did, for I loved her with all my heart; she was my pride and joy, but there came a time when I thought leaving was the only way to protect her."

"From grandmother?"

He nodded sadly. "Let me tell you the whole story."

"Would you like a little privacy," Brad asked. "If so, we'll walk over here out of earshot, but not so far that we can't see what's going on."

"It's okay, you can all stay," he said and started telling his story. "I was a young preacher, and I went from place to place, holding revival services. I was preaching in the town where your grandmother lived. She was the prettiest girl in town, probably in the whole state, and she was getting ready to compete for the state title, and then go on to the Miss America pageant, which she felt sure she would win." He paused to catch his breath. "She came to my revival and after the service ended, she came to the stage where I was getting my things together and started talking to me. She invited me to go out for something to drink at the local teen hang out. We went and had a great time, and we started going out every night after the service. Now, I would know better, but then I was young and foolish, and very flattered that such a beautiful girl would even notice me. One night when we were out very late, things got out of hand, and she ended up pregnant…"

"With mama," Cassie broke in.

He nodded. "Boy, was she mad! She accused me of getting her pregnant on purpose just so she could never become Miss America, because I wanted to keep her tied there to me. She was going to have an abortion, but I wouldn't let her. Abortions weren't legal then, and I threatened to turn her in if she tried to get rid of the baby. She ranted and raved, but I won, and the baby was saved. She hated me and said she never wanted to see me again, but her parents insisted that we get married, and since she was only seventeen, they forced her to marry me."

"Did you love her, Grandfather?" Cassie asked.

"No, not the way I should have," he answered with sadness in his voice. "But we got married and moved into a little house and waited for the baby to be born. When your mother was born, you're grandmother cursed me with every breath, during the entire birth. Then she never paid any attention to the baby. I had to name your mother. I named her Rebecca Lee, after my mother, and I took care of her, whenever I wasn't working. I gave up the ministry and got a regular job to support my family. I don't know how well your mother was taken care of when I was working. I always suspected that your grandmother didn't feed her or change her until right before I got home. She blamed the baby, along with me, for ruining her chances of becoming Miss America. She hated both of us. She would get mad at me and take it out on Rebecca by spanking her or taking toys away from her. When she saw how much this hurt me, things got worse. She wouldn't let your mother play at all, she would make her sit in a chair all day and do nothing, then, she started beating her for no reason, except to get back at me. I finally decided the only way I could put a stop to all this abuse was to leave. I reasoned that if I was not around, maybe she would stop taking things out on Rebecca."

"Why didn't you take her with you, Grandfather?"

"Your grandmother was the hometown girl and very highly respected. I was the unwelcome outsider who had tricked her into marrying me, and therefore foiled her plans, along with the town's plans, for her to become Miss America. They would have believed her, not me. I knew if I took Rebecca and left, they would track me down, and return her to her mother; and things would only be worse for her, so I left without my little girl. I've wondered through the years if I made the right choice."

"Grandmother never loved mama," Cassie said sadly. "She was mean to her, and when mama was fifteen, she ran off with a salesman who came through town."

"I'm so very sorry," he said. "If I could go back and do things over, I would stay and fight for my little girl. By the way, where is Rebecca? I suppose she lives here too."

"No, grandfather," Cassie said, and told him how the police officers had carried her mother away, and how she went on the run trying to find her, and ended up on the streets. "We don't know where mama is," she added, then, finished telling him everything.

"So that's why you jumped me," he said to Brad and the others. "Thank you for protecting my granddaughter. It's comforting to know she's in such good hands." Then he added, "I'd like to get my hands on the people who tried to hurt you, Cassie, and the ones who took your mother away."

"We are all praying that they will be found and punished," Brad said.

"What about my daughter, is Rebecca still alive?" His voice was strained, dreading to ask the question, dreading to hear the answer.

143

"The FBI and this friend of ours, a policeman in Nashville are sure of it," Brad said, trying to sound confident. "They believe it would be too risky for her to turn up dead; we're all praying that it turns out that way."

"What is being done to find her?"

"My daughter and her husband live in the area where Cassie and your daughter lived, so they're helping in the search," Ellis said. "If she's still in the area, they'll find her."

"Is there something I can do to help?"

"No, just wait and pray for the best," Brad said. "And, while you wait, why don't you stay here, so you can be close to your granddaughter?"

"I'd like that, but I don't want to impose. Is there a hotel close by?"

"Nonsense," Ellis replied. "There's plenty of family here for you to stay with, and you can help us in our vigil to keep Cassie safe."

"We have plenty of room here, and you're welcome to stay," Roseanna offered, "but, grandma has an extra bedroom; and it's close to where Cassie is staying. I'm sure she and the judge would be delighted to have you stay with them. That way you'd be close to Cassie all the time. I'll call grandma."

"Of course, we'll be happy to have him stay with us," Grandma assured her.

"Daddy will bring him over later," Roseana said. "Right now he needs to spend time with his granddaughter."

"Do you know where to find the wonderful little Baby that you told mama about?" Cassie asked. "I went looking for Him, but I couldn't find Him."

"Don't you know about God?" he asked, alarmed by her statement.

"God?" she questioned. "I've heard that name mentioned at Mr. Brad's church, but I've never seen him."

Her grandfather took her in his lap and told her about God, starting at the birth of Jesus and telling her the whole story. "God loves all of us so much…"

"God loves us?" she said, a look of disbelief on her face. "If He loves us so much, why did He let daddy beat up on mama and me, and why didn't he stop Duke's uncle from doing those bad things to him? If He can do anything, He could have stopped it, but He didn't---that doesn't sound like love to me. I don't think I like this God of yours, Grandfather."

Later, he would explain to her about the free will that God gave to humans so that we can choose whether to do good or evil; and, even though He hates it when evil men choose to hurt kids and others, He can't go back on His word, and take that free will away from them; but right now she wasn't ready to listen; right now she needed to feel loved, so he hugged her.

Chapter 17

Angelina's heart pounded wildly as she walked through the doors of the mental hospital. This was the first day of her assignment to observe and work with the mentally ill; and, her first day to work undercover. Fear seized her. Why had she agreed to do this; why had she not listened to Andy? It was easy to be brave when she was only talking about it; but now that she was actually here...She looked around. Were Chief Bristol's people here? Everyone looked as if they belonged, as if they had been here a long time. What if something had happened and they couldn't get them in place? What if she were on her own? Panic seized her and she wanted to turn and run.

A hand touched her shoulder. She jumped and a muffled cry came from her lips.

"I'm sorry, I didn't mean to startle you."

Angelina turned and looked into the face of a man, who appeared to be in his mid thirties, wearing a white doctor's coat. "No, I'm sorry," she said. "I guess I'm just a little jumpy."

"First day on the job jitters?"

"Something like that."

"Once you get used to things around here, you'll be okay," he told her.

"I'm just here for a few weeks as part of my training to become a doctor," she explained.

"Just my luck," he said. "I was hoping you'd be a permanent fixture around here. You sure do improve the scenery in this place."

She blushed. "Thank you," she said, accepting the compliment graciously.

A ringing sound interrupted their conversation. "I've got to be going," he said, looking at his pager. "I'm Doctor Blakely. If you need someone to show you the ropes, I'm here."

She thanked him and watched as he walked away. "Is he one of Chief Bristol's men?" she mused to herself. "Did he introduce himself and offer to help, in order to keep an eye on me?"

"Are you from the college?"

Angelina turned and saw a woman standing there. "Yes," she said, "I'm Angelina Winslow."

"I'm Mary Hopkins. I'm the administrator here. Follow me," she said. She showed Angelina to a room. "Wait in here. Someone will come and tell you what to do." She poured a cup of coffee and handed it to Angelina. "We didn't get too many students from the college to come here for training. You will be working, one on one, with one of our most qualified doctors. He's been here a while, so he knows his way around."

The door opened and a doctor walked in. "Hi again," he said, looking at Angelina and winking.

"Hello, Dr. Blakely," she replied, blushing slightly.

"You two know each other?"

"We met a little while ago in the lobby," he said, then turned and held out his hand to Angelina. "Looks like I *will* be showing you the ropes. I will be your tutor for as long as you're here."

"Great," she said, shaking his hand. She cringed inwardly, realizing there was no way he could be one of the agents sent here to protect her. What if he was in on this? What if he was one of them?

"I'm going on rounds now, would you like to go with me?"

She nodded and stood to her feet, a queasy feeling inside. Her job here was beginning. She wondered how it would end.

"Angelina, isn't it?" he inquired. "May I call you Angelina?"

"Yes sir, Dr. Blakely."

"Let's not be so formal," he said. "You can drop the sir part. Just call me Dr. Blakely."

"Yes, sir..." She blushed and mumbled that she was sorry.

"Loosen up," he said. "I'm not so bad once you get to know me."

"No, sir," she said, and blushed again.

He laughed. It was a good laugh and made Angelina feel more at ease. "Come on, let's get started," he said, handing her a pad and pen.

"This is Ms. Bette Davis," he said when they walked into a room where a woman with gobs of makeup all over her face was waiting.

"Hello, doc," she said. "Is my makeup on right? Do I look okay? That man from Hollywood is going to be here any minute now, and I have to look my best." She turned to Angelina. "Pretty thing, is my lipstick on straight?"

"Well, it could use a touch-up," Angelina said, grabbing a tissue and starting to rub it across the woman's face.

The woman slapped her hand away. "Get away! You're going to smudge my makeup!" she yelled. "I know what's going on here. You don't want that man from Hollywood to see me at my best. You want him to notice you. Get out of my room!"

Angelina stumbled out the door, tears welling up in her eyes. Her first time to observe the doctor at work and she had failed miserably.

He came out a few minutes later, a grin on his face. "That's lesson number one," he said. "You've got to know each patient. When some of them ask for your advice, they really only want your assurance."

"But her makeup was smeared all over her face," Angelina said, lamely. "What if she looked in a mirror? Wouldn't that devastate her more?"

"She's not allowed to have a mirror in her room," he said. "She thinks she's the beautiful actress, Bette Davis. You probably don't recognize that name; she was before your time...and mine," he added quickly.

"I'm sorry I messed things up," she said.

"You didn't mess anything up," he assured her. "Tomorrow, she won't remember any of this."

"I can see I've got a lot to learn," she muttered, writing on the pad.

"And, you won't learn it all in one day," he told her. "So, just be patient and, in time, it will come."

They went from room to room, visiting the patients. Angelina's heart went out to every one of them. She had a couple of propositions from two elderly men; one lady thought she was trying to steal her imaginary cat out of her room, still another accused her of having an affair with her husband. By the end of the day, she felt drained, and was ready to get out of that place, and get home to Andy.

Andy met her at the door with a kiss and she burst into tears. "What's wrong, honey?" he asked, concern in his voice.

"It was awful," she cried, and told him about the day she'd had working with Dr. Blakely. "Those poor people," she said. "My heart broke when I saw them in that condition. I don't think I could work with them every day the way Jeremy does..."

"So, now it's Jeremy?" Andy said, "What happened to Dr. Blakely?"

149

"He said since I was almost a fellow doctor that I should call him Jeremy, when we were not around patients."

"And, this Jeremy, what's he like?"

"He's very nice."

"He's also fat, bald and ugly, I hope," Andy remarked.

Angelina laughed. "No, actually, he's more the Prince Charming type; tall, dark and handsome, and very nice," she teased.

"I know the type," he groused. "You watch your step around him."

"Don't worry, baby, you're the only Prince Charming that I'm interested in; and I can take care of myself when it comes to other handsome, charming men. I just wish I was as capable when it comes to doing the job that I'm there to do."

"Did you make any headway today?"

She shook her head. "I didn't see anyone that vaguely resembled Cassie. We'll visit more of the rooms tomorrow. But, even if I find Rebecca, it's going to be hard to make contact with her, 'cause Dr. Blakely is always with me."

"You be careful, honey," he warned. "You don't know who you can trust in that place; this Dr. Blakely of yours could be a part of the slavery ring."

"I thought about that," she said. "I promise to watch my every step, and his too. Don't worry, sweetie, I'll be okay. Chief Bristol's people are there in case I run into trouble."

"Did you see any of them?"

She shook her head. "He said I wouldn't know who they are, that they would blend in with their surroundings and wouldn't be conspicuous. It makes me a little nervous not knowing who they are," she confessed. "One thing, I do know, Jeremy is not one of them; he's been there too long."

"I'm going to call Kent and make sure they are in place, and that you're very well protected," Andy said, picking up the phone and dialing. "I'm not going to let you risk your life."

"Thanks, baby," she said, snuggling close to him. She'd feel better knowing for sure the undercover agents were there, even if she didn't know who they were.

Andy showed up in the hospital cafeteria the next day. He spotted Angelina sitting at a table with a good-looking man. "Dr. Jeremy Blakely," he mumbled under his breath and walked over to where they were sitting.

Angelina looked up and saw him. "Andy," she exclaimed, happily, then, a cloud shadowed her face. "Why are you here, is something wrong?"

"No, baby, I just stopped by to have lunch with my beautiful wife," he explained. "I didn't realize you would go to lunch so early."

"That's my fault," the good doctor said, extending his hand. "We finished early so I suggested we come and get a bite to eat before tackling this afternoon's schedule. By the way, I'm Jeremy Blakely."

"Andy Winslow," Andy said, shaking the man's hand. "I'm Angelina's husband."

"I gathered that," the doctor said, smiling. "By all means, join us."

Andy stifled the urge to say what was on his mind; that he didn't have to be invited to join his wife for lunch. But aloud he said, "By the time I get through that long line the two of you will be finished and on your way back to work."

"Honey, you don't have to go through that line," Angelina told him. "I've got way too much food for me, so grab a fork and share my dinner."

"Are you sure, baby?" he asked, really wanting to get a chance to check the good doctor out.

She nodded and Andy hurried over, grabbed a fork, and joined them.

"Would the two of you like some privacy?" Dr. Blakely asked.

"No, of course not," Andy quickly answered. "This is a good time to get acquainted." The conversation was a bit strained, with Andy asking Dr. Blakely all kinds of personal questions.

The doctor put up his hand. "What is this? Am I on trial or something?"

Angelina blushed, and gave Andy a sharp kick on the shin. "My husband is very protective of me," she explained, "especially when I'm working with such a good looking man."

It was Andy's turn to blush. "I'm sorry," he said. "I apologize to you, doctor, and to my wife; I'm not usually so rude. She described you as the Prince Charming type, tall, dark and handsome; so, I figured I'd better come down and check you out. Will you forgive me?"

Dr. Blakely laughed heartily. "Well, you're honest, to say the least. I don't blame you, if I had a wife that looks like your wife, I'd be protective of her too."

Andy wanted to ask if he was married, but he thought he'd better not; he was in enough trouble with Angelina already.

They changed the subject and the rest of the lunch hour went by smoothly. Andy even caught himself almost liking the doctor.

"I'm sorry I embarrassed you, baby," he whispered to Angelina as he kissed her goodbye.

"We'll talk about it when I get home," she whispered, and kissed him back.

"Tall, dark and handsome, huh? The Prince Charming type?" Jeremy teased, as they walked down the hall together. "My day is looking up already."

Angelina blushed but didn't answer him.

Andy and Angelina had their first real fight when she got home that afternoon. "How dare you come to my workplace and check up on me, and then tell Jeremy that I said he was good-looking..."

"I believe you used those words first," Andy said in defense of his actions. "I only repeated what you said."

"Well, you should have kept your comments to yourself," she said. "Now, I'll never be able to make him stop flirting with me."

"I knew he was that kind of man," Andy snorted. "Angelina, if he tries something, I'll..."

She pulled him into her arms and kissed him. "I can handle him," she said. "But, I love you for being jealous, you silly, wonderful man."

He kissed her and the fight was over.

"Did Kent get in touch with Chief Bristol," she asked.

"Yes, and he assured him that his people are all in place, and that you don't make a move that they don't know about."

Angelina had been at the hospital for a week now, and she had not found the slightest clue that Cassie's mother was being held here. They were going to the west wing to work today.

"Aren't we going in there?" she asked, as they passed by one of the rooms.

"I don't go in there much," he answered. "The lady in there is a Jane Doe, and there's not much I can do for her. She just lays and stares, never has a reaction of any kind." He paused thoughtfully. "I think we will go in there today. It will be good practice for you, in case you run into someone like her later."

They walked into the darkened room. Dr. Blakely turned the light on.

Angelina clasped her hand over her mouth to keep from crying out. The woman lying there, hopeless and only

153

half alive, looked just like Cassie. She had found Rebecca Bowman; she was sure of it.

"Are you all right," the doctor asked, hearing her muffled cry and seeing the expression on her face.

Angelina had to think quickly. "Yes," she said. "She just looks so sad and alone, it threw me for a minute. How long has she been like this?"

"Since the day they brought her in," he said. "Poor woman, I don't guess she has a family; no one ever comes to see her."

Tears rolled down Angelina's face. "I wish there was a way I could bring some sunshine into her life; put a spark of hope in her eyes."

"I don't think anything would reach her," he said, a bit sadly. "And, Angelina, you can't let things like this bother you. You have to be objective or you'll go crazy in this kind of work." He took the woman's hands in his and looked down at her compassionately. "If there was only someway I could reach you." He let go of her hands and they walked out of the room.

When they had gone a few feet down the hall, Angelina stopped. "I left my pad and pen in there. You go on ahead, I'll go back for it," she said, hoping he didn't insist on going with her. She'd left her things behind as an excuse to be alone with the woman, and try to find out if she truly was Cassie's mother.

He pointed to a room close by. "I'll be in there," he said.

Angelina walked into the room and over to the bed. She turned the small light on beside the bed. She took the woman's hand. "Cassie," she said, hoping the woman would respond. Nothing. "Cassie," she said, a little louder.

The woman's hand moved inside Angelina's. Life twinkled in her eyes. "Cassie," she whispered in a voice that was weak and anguished.

"Cassie is okay," Angelina told her. "She's with my family and they are taking really good care of her. She's safe there with them. Listen carefully. We're going to get you out of here and take you to your daughter, so just hang on a little longer, and don't let on that I was here, or your life could be in more danger. I've got to go now, but I'll be back, I promise." She leaned over and kissed her, picked up the pad and pen, and left the room.

"I found her," she cried excitedly, that afternoon when she got home. "Andy, I found Cassie's mother," she cried again, running into his arms and sobbing joyously.

Chapter 18

"Did Jesse and you have a fight when you were in New Orleans?" Roseanna asked bluntly, the next day when she went to see Belle, with Earl along as a bodyguard. He sat in the car to make sure no strangers were hanging around.

"Did we ever," Belle said. "Actually, I did all the fighting; Jesse was on the receiving end. I mixed his steak sauce with Louisiana hot sauce and cayenne pepper, and then I hit him with my hairdryer."

"But why, Belle?"

"I learned some things about Pamela and Jesse that hurt me deeply," Belle said, "and I wanted to hurt him the way he hurt me. I got my revenge all right but it sure wasn't sweet."

"How did Jesse react?"

"He was gentle and understanding like he always is."

"Did you get things worked out?"

"Not entirely. I know Jesse loves me with all his heart and I love him the same," she said, "but after finding out the special things he did with Pamela, I felt like I wasn't special to him and never had been; it hurt me deeply, and I can't deal with it yet. He understands all this and he suggested moving into the guest room until I can work though it. He realizes that he never did anything special for me, so he's planning a trip to Hawaii for us as soon as things are right between us again."

Roseanna hugged her. "Honey, that sounds great," she said. "Brad and I will pray for you and Jesse, and we'll keep this between the four of us," she promised. "Can you imagine what would happen if daddy found out?"

"I don't want to go there again, considering what happened last time."

"I don't blame you," Roseanna said, laughing.

"Is that Earl I saw in the car with you? Why didn't he come in?"

"He came along as my bodyguard," Roseanna explained.

"Bodyguard?" Belle asked, raising her eyebrows.

"I need to talk to you about that," Roseanna said, explaining the danger she had put all of them in because of the shopping trip with Isabelle and Cassie.

"I don't think we will be in any danger here in town," Belle said, "but if you need us there to help out, Jesse is pretty good with a gun."

"We've got plenty of help, now, but if we should need you, I'll let you know."

"It would be normal for the picture to make the Nashville paper, with the concert coming up," Belle pointed out, "but do you really think it made the newspapers in other cities?"

Roseanna nodded. "I'm sure of it," she said. "A man, that lived in New York City, showed up at our house yesterday, looking for Cassie, saying that he'd seen the picture in the paper."

"What happened?"

"Brad grabbed him and Earl threatened to shoot his head off, but, he turned out to be Cassie's grandfather, so there was no problem; but if he saw the picture, the bad guys could have seen it too, and that could put all of us in danger, so we have doubled our guard on both our house and mama's."

"That settles it," Belle said. "As soon as Jesse gets home from work, we're coming out there, and, we'll stay until this mess is over."

157

"Thanks, sis," Roseanna said, kissing Belle and walking out the door.

All the family was gathered at Roseanna's when Belle, Jesse and the kids arrived late that afternoon.

"Come on in, we're having a family supper," Brad called as they got out of the car.

They were just about to sit down for supper, when the phone rang. Mama was close by, so she answered it. She listened a moment then let out a yell of excitement. "Cassie, Angelina wants to talk to you, she's found your mother!"

Cassie ran to the phone. "You found mama?"

"Yes, Cassie, I found her."

"Can I come home? Can I see her?"

"No, baby, not yet," Angelina said. "She's here in a mental hospital, and we have to find a way to get her out. So you need to stay put for a little while longer. I promise you, we will get her out and bring her to you."

"When?"

"I don't know, we have to make plans and be very careful," Angelina said. "If they suspect anything is going on your mother could be in a lot of danger."

"Is mama okay?"

"They're keeping her heavily sedated, but I believe she's okay."

"Thanks, Angelina, for finding her, and, if you can, would you tell her that Grandfather Cassidy is here with me."

"Her father? I'll try to find a way to let her know. That will give her even more reason to hang in there."

The tears flowed freely as everyone hugged Cassie and shouts of joy filled the room.

"We're not out of the woods yet, the most dangerous part is just beginning," Brad reminded them. "Angelina could be in a lot of danger along with Cassie's mother, if they get caught; so as soon as we finish supper, let's all go to the church and pray for their safety."

"The rest of you go to the church," Ellis stated. "I'm going to Friends Harbor. I'm going to be there for Angelina. I'm going to protect my daughter…"

"Ellis, you can't do that," Mama said. "You'd go off on one of your tangents and get Angelina hurt for sure. You're going to let the people who know what they're doing handle it; you're going to stay right here and pray like the rest of us."

"She's right, Ellis," Brad said. "As much as all of us would like to be there, all we can do is stay here and pray; and I believe that prayer is the most powerful weapon we can have right now."

Angelina handed the phone to Andy. "Honey, you call Kent. He will want to get in touch with Chief Bristol as soon as possible. I only have two more weeks at the hospital, so we need to make plans."

"Honey, is there anyway you can get out of that place right now, and let the FBI handle getting her out? I don't want you to put yourself in harms way."

"No, I have to finish my time there if I want to graduate," she said. "We'll let Chief Bristol decide the best way to get her out."

Andy put in the call to Nashville. Kent was delighted to hear that Rebecca Bowman had been found. He promised to call the chief and have him get in touch with them.

The call from the chief came some thirty minutes later. "Congratulations, Mrs. Winslow. You did a great job."

"Thank you sir," Angelina answered. "I'm glad I could do it."

"Now, your people take over from here, right?" Andy asked, listening in on another phone.

"I wish I could say yes, Mr. Winslow, but, your wife still has the best chance to get the Bowman woman out of the hospital safely," the chief told him. "She has access to that room that my agents would not have. As I understand it she works closely with a doctor by the name of Jeremy Blakely, and therefore can come and go with a fairly free rein. We can use this to our advantage."

"What about my wife? Can you guarantee me that she will be safe?"

"There are no absolute guarantees," Chief Bristol answered, honestly. "But I can promise you that she will be protected as much as is humanly possible. If we feel at any time that your wife's life is in danger we will abort the operation."

Angelina had been listening in and she spoke up, "Chief, what did you have in mind. How do we go about this?"

"I want your ideas on the best way and time to snatch her from the hospital," he said. "This is going to be tricky, and if it is to succeed, we must plan it down to the split second. There will be no room for error." He hesitated a moment. "Do you think I can come to your house where we can work on a plan together?"

"We can send my father's company jet to pick you up," Andy said. "The pilot has worked for our family for years, and he can be trusted. A friend of ours will pick you up at the airport and bring you here. That way there should be no problems. And, you can stay with us as long as necessary."

"Thank you, Mr. Winslow," the chief said. "How soon can we get started?"

"The jet is here," Andy said. "The pilot can be on his way as soon as he files the flight plans. Where should he pick you up?"

"I'm in Nashville now, so he can fly into the airport here. I'll be waiting."

160

"Okay," Andy told him. "As soon as I know the flight plans I'll call Kent and he can get in touch with you. The man that picks you up at the airport here is named Carlos, and he will be driving a cab. How will he recognize you?"

"I'll be wearing a flashy western suit with a big ten gallon hat and flashy alligator boots. My dress attire will scream 'rich Texas billionaire,' all the way; no one would take me for an FBI agent. He will walk up to me and say: "Had any gushers lately?" and I will answer loudly: "Only a couple of thousand, boy." That way no one will get suspicious. If I try to sneak in, and someone is watching, they would be sure to notice and wonder what I have to hide. Sometimes the best way to hide something is to put it out in plain sight."

"I'll fill Carlos in and he will be waiting for you."

"Okay, I'll see you soon."

Chapter 19

Chief Bristol made a quick change of clothes in the taxi, while Carlos drove around the long way in order to throw off anyone that might be following them.

"Carlos sure does like all this mysterious stuff," he remarked. "My life was dull before I met Senor Andy and the beautiful Angelina. Now I am driving a real FBI man to their house. America is so wonderful."

"Wouldn't you get this opportunity in Mexico?" Chief Bristol asked.

Carlos shook his head. "In the village where I live only the big-wigs get opportunities; that's why Carlos come to America."

Looking behind them, and satisfied that no one was following, the chief told Carlos to pull into the parking lot of Andy's apartment house. He then thanked him, and walked up the backstairs. It was the middle of the night, so he was sure that no one spotted him. He tapped lightly on Andy's door.

Andy was waiting up and opened the door immediately. "Come in, Chief," he said. "I'm Andy Winslow. Kent has told us a lot about you and I'm happy to finally meet you."

"Hello, son," the chief said warmly. "Kent has told me a lot about you and your lovely wife, and I am happy to be meeting the two of you."

"I sent Angelina on to bed," Andy said. "She has an early day tomorrow and I want to make sure she's up to it."

"That's good," the chief answered. "We want her to be on her toes every minute that she's in that hospital."

"How was your flight, sir?" Andy asked, getting bed linens from the closet.

"Perfect," he answered.

"We only have one bedroom, but this couch sleeps pretty good," Andy said, spreading the covers on the couch. "Tomorrow we'll buy a roll-away bed for you."

"The couch will be fine," Chief Bristol said, "Now, where is the bathroom?"

Angelina had to leave for work early next morning so they only had time for quick introductions.

"I'll come up some tentative plans, and when you get home, we can look them over and see which ones will work and what needs to be added."

Angelina's day did not start out good. The first patient was old Mr. Jones, whom she had nicknamed 'the pincher'. She had to move fast to stay out of his reach. The only good thing about coming into this room was that it was across the hall from Rebecca's room, so that meant they would be going there next. She had to think of a way to let her know about Cassie and her father.

"Ouch!" she yelled, as Mr. Jones caught her off guard and gave her a big pinch. "Stop that," she scolded, looking at Dr. Blakely for help.

The doctor grinned and shook his head. "I'd change places with Mr. Jones, in a minute, if I could get away with the pinching," he teased.

"Men," she said, contempt in her voice, and made sure she stayed out of pinching distance of Mr. Jones.

"You sure didn't help any in there," she scolded as they walked out into the hallway.

Dr. Blakely laughed. "That old man is harmless."

"Only because I can outrun him," she said, then, put it out of her mind as they walked into Rebecca's room.

"How's my patient today?" the doctor asked, taking her hand and feeling her pulse. "Her pulse is a little stronger. That's a good sign." He checked her other vitals, nodding his head. "She is making some improvement."

"That's great," Angelina replied, realizing that she had gotten through to Rebecca over the past few days, telling her not to take all the medication they were giving her. "Good girl," she whispered, leaning close to the woman's ear.

"We'll stop by a couple of more rooms before we go to lunch," Dr. Blakely said as he finished examining her. "Someday soon maybe she can respond, and we can get inside her mind and find out what's bothering her."

"Is it okay if I stay in here a minute and fluff up her pillows and try to make her a little more comfortable?"

"Of course," he said. "I need to stop by the desk anyway, so I'll meet you in room 30."

Angelina talked in a soft voice as she fluffed the pillows. "Rebecca, I told Cassie that we found you and that you are okay. She was so happy. She loves you and can't wait to see you again. I told her we're working on getting you out of here and getting the two of you back together. And, your father, Frank Cassidy, is there with Cassie, and he is very anxious to see you, too. So, hang in there, and don't let on that I've told you anything. Your life will depend on keeping all of this a secret."

Rebecca batted her eyes and smiled faintly, letting Angelina know that she understood. Angelina kissed her and left the room, to join Dr. Blakely for the rest of the morning rounds.

Andy and Chief Bristol were waiting when she got home late that afternoon. Andy gave her a big welcome home kiss.

"Thanks, I needed that," she said.

"Bad day, huh," Andy asked, rubbing her neck.

"Huh-um, starting with that awful Mr. Jones, the pincher."

"He pinched you?" Andy asked. "How old is that creep?"

"He's at least in his eighties, but he fancies himself a real Romeo."

"I'll be glad when you're out of that place," Andy groused. "First that wolf that calls himself a doctor, now an eighty year old Casanova."

"I'm sorry to ignore you, Chief Bristol," she said, extending her hand to him. "I just needed to unwind."

He grinned impishly. "I'm sorry, but I have this picture in my mind of that old man chasing you around the room trying to pinch you."

"Let's forget about him, and get down to business," she said. "We've got to come up with a way to get Rebecca out of there quick, before anyone gets suspicious."

"I have some plans drawn up, as far as our end is concerned, but we have to figure out how to handle the inside work, actually getting her out of there. That's where you come in," he said, spreading out some papers on the table. "My people have surveyed the hospital grounds and we feel this would be the best place to pick her up," he added, pointing to a street lined with trees and bushes. "We can park there with less chances of being noticed. The problem is getting her to the car."

Angelina nodded. "That place is well guarded; how are we going to get her out of there without getting caught?"

"What would be the best time to try this?" the chief asked. "A time when less people will be around?"

Angelina thought a moment. "Probably the noon hour," she said. "Most of the staff takes their lunch break between twelve and one o'clock; and, the ones who are left there have so much to do that they don't have time to watch everything that goes on."

The noon hour, it is," Chief Bristol said, writing that down in his notes. "Now, how do we get her out?"

165

"I usually eat lunch with Jeremy in the cafeteria, but I could beg off, because, I will have a date to eat lunch with my wonderful husband; then I can sneak into her room with a wheelchair, and wheel her out the back way, and over to the car, where you are waiting."

"That sounds simple enough," the chief said, "but, we've got to tear the plan apart; look at it from every angle, analyze every possible thing that could go wrong, and find a way to combat against each one; only then will we even consider it. I'll need a few days to go over this with my people and work out the bugs. We have to know that every base is covered and the margin for error is zero."

Chief Bristol got in touch with his people working undercover at the hospital, as well as his advisors in the main office; they put theirs heads together and in a couple of days had worked out a plan they felt sure was foolproof. It included Angelina's idea on how to sneak Rebecca out during the lunch hour. They would put the plan in action on Friday, the last day of Angelina's time at the hospital. No one would notice until time for Rebecca's medicine that night that she was missing. Angelina would already be gone, and hopefully no one would associate her with the woman's disappearance, since if everything went as planned, no one would see her leave the hospital with Cassie's mother.

After the plans were finalized and everything was set on go, Andy called Brad and told him how it was all going down. "We need your prayers," he said. "I'm not totally in favor of this, but Angelina has made up her mind to do it, and as you know when one of the LeBlanc girls decide to do something, there's no changing them."

"I know," Brad said. He had dealt with not just one, but all of the LeBlanc girls through the years, and he had learned better than to try to change their minds. "I'll get the entire congregation, here, to pray through the whole noon hour on Friday," he promised. "Is there anything else we can do?"

"No," Andy said. "I can't even do anything, and it's driving me crazy, just having to sit back and wait, while my wife's life is put in jeopardy."

"Hang in there," Brad told him. "We've got to believe that God will be there with Angelina, watching over her, and, He can do a better job than any of us could."

"Thanks, Brad," Andy said, and hung up the phone, still worried and upset that Angelina was walking into danger and there was no way he could help her. "Brad's right. Prayer is the only answer," he muttered, falling to his knees.

Chapter 20

Friday dawned bright and clear. At least the weather was cooperating. Angelina was not faring so well. She woke up early, nervous and jumpy. Today could be the last day of her life if she got caught trying to sneak Rebecca out of the hospital. She awoke before Andy and Chief Bristol and made a big pot of coffee, hoping that would calm her down before she had to face them. She wished she had more faith, like Roseanna and Belle; but she had not fully surrendered to the values of being brought up in church like they had; she had always looked out for herself; now she wished she had learned to depend on God more; she sure could use Him today. Andy had a lot of faith, but would that count for her?

Chief Bristol walked into the kitchen, poured himself a cup of coffee and sat down at the breakfast bar. "How are you holding up, Angelina?" He saw that she was trembling. "Last minute jitters?"

She nodded. "Don't tell Andy," she said. "He'd never allow me to go through with it."

"Are you sure you want to?" the Chief asked, concern in his voice. "It's not too late to call this off."

"No, I'll be all right," she said. "We're going ahead as planned. I want to help rescue Cassie's mother 'cause if we don't stop those creeps they will keep on doing all the terrible things they've been doing, and Cassie and her mother are the only ones who can stop them, right?"

"Well, without Cassie and her mother we don't have much of a case against that bunch of scum; they will probably walk free, and keep on doing the same thing to other kids."

"Well, let's get them," Angelina said, just as Andy walked in. She walked over and kissed him.

"How's my girl holding up?" he asked, pulling her into his arms and holding her close.

"I'm fine, now, here in your arms. Andy, you make me feel so safe."

"That settles it," he said, "you're not going through with this. The deals off."

"Andy, think back to how angry you were when you rescued Cassie from that man," Angelina said tearfully. "Honey, there are lots of little kids who don't get rescued and who are living in pure hell everyday because of what these perverts are doing, and I want to help put a stop to them." Tears were rolling down her face.

"Baby, are you sure you can do this?" he asked, nervously.

"With you and the folks back home praying for me, how can I miss?" Her words were brave, but she was scared to death on the inside.

"Angelina, remember, you won't be alone, I have over a dozen agents surrounding you and watching you; they are ready to move in at a moments notice."

"Okay, let's do it," she said, giving Andy a goodbye kiss and nodding to the chief.

Angelina and Dr. Blakely made their rounds as they did every morning; but things were different today; Dr. Blakely was excited because this was Friday and he had a big weekend planned; Angelina was nervous, hoping that she would still have a weekend when this was all over.

She kept looking at her watch, halfway wishing she could stop time, and 12:00 o'clock noon would never get here.

"What's wrong with you, Angelina, you seem as nervous as a cat," the good doctor remarked. "Did you have a fight with your husband, or did your mother-in-law drop in unexpectedly?"

"No, nothing like that," she assured him. "I didn't sleep well last night and I'm a little jittery."

"Come on, it's time to visit your favorite patient," he said, teasingly, as they walked into the room of old Mr. Jones.

"He'd better not try anything, today," she scowled.

"I need my pillows fluffed," the old man said, looking at Angelina. She ignored him. "Here, you need to feel my forehead," he said, again looking at her. "I think I got fever..."

"Your nurse will give you something for that fever," Angelina answered, keeping her distance.

"Let's look in on Jane Doe before we stop for lunch," the doctor suggested, as they left Mr. Jones' room. "What's this wheelchair doing out in the hallway," he commented, a little put out. "A patient could fall over it and get hurt."

"Here, I'll put it in this room, out of the way, until someone can move it," Angelina said, pushing the wheelchair into a corner in Rebecca's room. She knew that one of the undercover agents had put it in the hallway for her to use later.

"Well, I guess that's it," he said, as he finished examining the woman. "She seems to be improving a little every day; and I think it has something to do with you; the special attention you've given her. No one else has done that. It's paying off." He took Angelina's hand. "Are you sure you don't want to change your field of medicine and come work here with me?"

"I have enjoyed working with you," she said, "and I've certainly learned a lot about human nature."

"Especially from Mr. Jones," he laughed.

"I sure won't miss having to dodge his advances every day."

"He may be old, but he sure hasn't lost his eyesight," the doctor said. "He knows beauty when he sees it, and what harm does a little pinch now and then do?"

"You're just as bad as he is," she said, "only difference is; you know I'd slap your face."

"And, it would be worth it," he said grinning. "Seriously, Angelina, if you ever get tired of that husband of yours..."

"I won't," she said, flatly, closing the subject.

"It's time for me to get out of here," he said, looking at his watch. "Have a nice lunch with your husband, and I'll see you in a couple of hours."

She watched until he turned the corner out of sight. She carefully pulled Rebecca into the wheelchair and wrapped a blanket around her. The plan had started. Her heart was pounding furiously, but she was doing everything she was supposed to do, she was right on schedule, the way they had planned it. She pushed the wheelchair out into the hall. The hallway was empty---too empty. Where were Chief Bristol's people? The one's who were supposed to protect her, they were nowhere in sight. Old Mr. Jones was taking it all in from his bed across the hall. Would he remember seeing her take Rebecca out of the room, would he tell? She couldn't worry about that; she had to get out of here. She had pushed the wheelchair a few feet down the hall when a hand touched her shoulder.

"What are you doing?" a voice demanded. "Where are you taking that woman?"

She recognized the voice even before she turned to face Dr. Blakely.

She looked around for help, but no one was there. She was on her own. Was he one of them? If so, she was caught already, but if not, maybe he would listen to reason. "I'm-a-taking-her-a-out for some fresh air," she mumbled feebly.

171

"On whose authority?" he snapped. "I never gave any such orders. Now tell me what's really going on."

"I've got to get her out of here, please, don't try to stop me," she pleaded. "It's a matter of life or death."

"I don't know what you're talking about, but I won't let you leave this hospital with my patient. I'm calling security and we'll get to the bottom of this." He pulled out his phone.

"You touch that dial and you're a dead man," a voice said, as a gun was jabbed in the doctor's back.

"Old Mr. Jones?" Angelina said, not believing what she was seeing. "You're a federal agent?"

"At your service, ma-am," he said, bowing low. "But we don't have time for small talk, we've got to get her out of here." He took over and began giving orders. "Doctor, you push the wheelchair. Angelina, you hold on to me, since I'm old and feeble and can't walk without help. Dr. Blakely, my gun will be pointed at you at all times, and I will shoot, if you don't do exactly what I tell you."

"Who are you people and what are you doing," the doctor asked, nervously.

"Never mind, just follow orders and everything will be fine," Mr. Jones said. "We're going out the back way, so hopefully we won't meet anyone, but if we should, you tell them, that you're taking the patients out for some fresh air. Did you fix the covers so it will look like she is sleeping?"

"Yes," Angelina replied, "Now, let's get out of here."

"Hold on to me tight, girlie," the agent posing as Mr. Jones, muttered in the voice of an eighty year old.

"You behave yourself," she scowled, "We're going to talk about those pinches when this is over."

"Just trying to keep in character," he said, winking at her.

They went through the back hall, down to the basement, without anyone seeing them; now they only had to go out the door and walk across the lawn without drawing undue attention. There were people milling around the grounds of the hospital, but none of them seemed to notice what was going on. They reached the car where Chief Bristol and the other agents were waiting.

One of the men jumped out of the car and lifted Rebecca out of the wheelchair and into the back seat. He got in beside her and shut the door.

"Now, may I go?" Dr. Blakely asked, nervously.

"No, you're coming with us," the chief said. "We can't take any chances with you. You're going to make some phone calls to let the staff know that you are going to take the rest of the day off..."

"That's already taken care of," the doctor said. "That's what I came back to tell you, Angelina. I had taken the afternoon off for both you and me. So your tenure at the hospital is over. You don't have to go back," he explained. "Now, I insist that you tell me what's going on here."

This is Chief Bristol of the FBI and he will explain everything," Angelina said. "Now you've got to get out of here, and I've got to meet my wonderful husband for lunch. Goodbye and good luck," she called as the car pulled away.

She hurried over to Andy's car. "It's done," she exclaimed, getting into the front seat and scooting over close to him, needing to feel the safety of his arms. "Chief Bristol and his men have Rebecca, and, are on their way to the airport. Now, let's get out of here."

"Where to?"

"Honey, let's go home," she said. "I need to be home right now. I need you to hold me. Andy, I was so scared; and things didn't go like they were supposed to," she cried, and told him the whole story.

"You mean that creep, Mr. Jones, is not an eighty year old man, he's an agent?" How old is he?"

"I'm not sure, but he sure gets around fast when he has to. He was there with the gun in Jeremy's back, before either one of us saw him."

"I'm going to have a little one on one talk with him about pinching my wife," Andy said, angrily. "Do you think Dr. Blakely is part of the slavery ring?"

"I don't think so," she answered thoughtfully. "He seemed genuinely in the dark about everything. I really hope he's not a part of it."

"I'll fix some lunch," Andy said, when they got home a few minutes later.

"Okay, while you do that, I'll call mama. I know they're so worried." She dialed the phone. She waited for an answer. "Please, be there, Mama," she whispered.

"Hello," a voice finally answered.

"Mama, it's over," she cried into the phone. "Rebecca is free, she's with the FBI. They're taking her someplace where she'll be safe..."

"How about you, baby, are you okay?"

"Yes, Mama, I'm fine. I'm here with Andy."

"It's over," Blanche yelled to the folks gathered there, praying for Angelina's safety and for the safety of all those involved. "Cassie, your mother is out of that hospital and safe in the care of the FBI."

Angelina could hear shouts of joy in the background, as mama told them the good news. "I'm back, Angelina," Mama said, "I just had to tell the folks here that it's over and you're okay. Do you want me to call the others and tell them?"

"Yes, Mama," she said. "I just want to sit here with Andy and try to unwind and put this ordeal out of my mind; at least for a while."

Mama called Roseanna to tell them the news. There were several people gathered there praying. Brad answered the phone. "Praise the Lord," he shouted when he heard the message. "Thanks, Mama," he said and hung up. "It's over!" he yelled to the others. "Angelina got Rebecca out and they're both safe. The FBI has Cassie's mother, and they are taking her to a place where she'll be safe. Angelina is at home with Andy and he's taking good care of her." Brad tried to sound confident, concerning Andy and Angelina, but he knew they were not out of the woods yet. Angelina had to stay there until she graduated next week; and if that bunch of perverts even suspected that she had anything to do with Rebecca's disappearance, then, she and Andy might not get out alive. "Oh, God, continue to watch over them," he prayed.

Andy held Angelina close as he felt her tremble in his arms. "It's over, baby, you're safe now."

"For how long, Andy?" she asked. "When they discover that Rebecca is missing they're going to start looking around to see who is responsible. What if the trail leads straight to me? What are we going to do then? How will we protect ourselves? What if they decide to get rid of us?"

"Shhh," he whispered. "It's going to be okay, honey. Chief Bristol left some of his people behind to keep an eye on us and make sure we're safe." He was trying to reassure his wife; he just wished he felt sure, and this queasy feeling in the pit of his stomach would go away.

Chapter 21

Pauline Nelson nervously turned the ring on her finger, as she glanced at the big clock, hanging on the wall in the Office of Social Services where she worked. The big man from New York City would be here in a few minutes and there would be hell to pay.

One would hardly recognize her as the harsh stern social worker she portrayed everyday in her line of work. Her short brown hair was curled and lay full around her face, softening her features. She was wearing a long slim skirt, in a soft green print, with a solid green top that caught the green in her eyes and put a sparkle in them that usually wasn't there. She had spent over an hour, applying the right make-up. She wanted to look just right tonight, hoping the big boss would notice the change, like what he saw, and maybe go easier on them.

She was joined by Mary Hopkins, administrator at the hospital, along with Mack Sanders, the chief of police, and several of his officers.

"What happened?" she asked Mary, hoping to get some answers before the big man got here, but before the other lady could answer, the door opened, and the man from New York City walked in.

"I want some answers," he stormed, "and they better be good!" He was tall, slightly on the frail side, with tender brown eyes, that covered up his real character. Those who worked closely with him weren't fooled by his kindly features; they knew him for the ruthless man that he was. "Come on, speak up!" he demanded sharply, when, not one of them offered to answer him. "Miss Nelson, you're in charge here, so you explain to me how an almost comatose woman was able to leave the hospital and disappear into thin air?"

"We're still looking into that, sir," she answered, turning the ring on her finger again.

"Miss Hopkins, can you shed some light on the matter?" he asked, glaring at her with anger in his eyes.

She swallowed hard. "We-a-found some pills that she had stuffed under the mattress, so I guess she-a-wasn't as heavily sedated as we thought."

"Who had access to the woman?"

"Dr. Blakely, of course..."

"Do you trust him?"

"Yes, he's been there for years, and nothing like this has ever happened."

"Was there anyone else who had access to her?"

"Only his assistant, the young student from medical school."

"His assistant, tell me more about her," he ordered.

"Her name is Angelina Winslow and her husband is the son of one of the richest men in the country---as in Winslow Steel." Miss Hopkins answered. "It was on Dr. Blakely's report that the woman he knew only as Jane Doe, was making improvement, and he gave all the credit to Mrs. Winslow, saying that she showed special attention to the patient."

The man cursed angrily. "That's all we need, a wealthy do-gooder. She must have thought the Bowman woman wasn't getting proper care here, and sneaked her out right from under your noses," he snapped. "They probably have her hidden away in a very private exclusive clinic; one that we can't get within a mile of." He cursed again and turned to a young man that had come with him to the meeting, "Can you tap into the college computer files and get all the information on this Angelina Winslow?"

"Can do, boss," he answered. "It will take a while to get in, but when it comes to computers, there's nothing hid there that I can't find."

"While he's doing that, we need to discuss another subject, the woman's daughter, and, the fact that she also eluded all of you, including this town's finest," the man commented, in a slow deliberate tone, looking over at the officers. "She was eleven, right? Can you tell me how an eleven-year-old kid could outfox all of you for months, then, how she was sold to one of our best clients, and managed to get away from him too, and ended up there?" He shoved the newspaper article concerning Roseanna and the girls in their faces. "I want some answers!" he demanded furiously, pounding his fist on the table.

"I had it all planned out," Miss Nelson explained. "The officers who took the Bowman woman away were not a part of this, so I told them that I had a foster home that would take the little girl that evening, then I waited for over an hour, but she didn't show up."

"That means you waited for over an hour to start looking for her. Didn't you realize she could be in the next county by then?" The man shook his head. "And, about her escaping from the man you sold her to…"

"She scalded his face," Miss Nelson blurted out.

"She's quite a resourceful little girl," the man stated. "Too bad, she's not a part of our team, instead of the likes of you. What about the man, she must have given the cops a description of him."

"We got him safely out of the country so he won't be a problem," the chief of police told him.

"Forget wealthy do-gooder," the young man at the computer exclaimed. "Look what I found here in the files. Mrs. Winslow is the former Angelina LeBlanc from south Louisiana; the superstar, Roseanna, lives there; her name was also LeBlanc, and, that's where the girl is."

178

"Do we see a pattern emerging here?" the big man asked, sarcastically.

"They probably carried Mrs. Bowman there, and that could work to our advantage," Miss Nelson pointed out. "We can go there and take care of both of them at the same time."

The man shook his head. "Stupid thinking; that's what got us into this mess in the first place," he said. "Did it ever occur to you that they have realized we probably saw the picture and know that the girl is there? Don't you think they will take steps to insure her safety? They will have her so heavily guarded that it would be suicide to try to get to her."

"What can we do?" Miss Nelson asked, sheepishly.

The man thought a moment. "We wait 'til the concert," he said. "Unless I miss my guess, they will all go to Nashville since it will be easier to guard them, if they are all together. Of course, I will have one of my men snoop around the bayou country to make sure they will all attend."

"But, how can we get to the little girl at the concert; she will surely be surrounded by guards there," Chief Sanders pointed out.

"What's the best way to get rid of guards?" the man asked, then, answered his own question. "By drawing their attention to something else."

"How do we do that?" the chief asked.

"What would happen if one of the performers on stage got shot?"

"Everyone would rush to his or her side," the young computer expert exclaimed, and then gasped, "You don't mean shoot Roseanna..."

"Or the kid," the man said, "it's says here in the article that Roseanna's daughter will be singing that night, too. And, everyone would rush to a kid's aid. That would leave the coast clear to get the Bowman girl."

"That might take care of Cassie, but what about her mother?" Miss Nelson asked.

"By herself, the mother can't hurt us," the man explained. "She was legally admitted to that hospital, right?"

Miss Nelson nodded. "We have all the bases covered there."

"Then we don't have to worry about her. But, we've got to get our hands on the kid. She can point the finger at this department for taking her mother away; and, she can testify how she was sold to that man to be used in pornography. If she ever puts the two together, we're in big trouble. As of now, no one has associated any of this with the department and we're going to keep it that way." He paused, as a knowing look covered his face. "If the kid talks, the evidence will only point to your local department, not to the rest of us; and, you are all dispensable."

"You wouldn't kill us," Miss Nelson exclaimed, horrified.

"This is a multi-billion dollar operation and I will not allow it to be brought down by an eleven year old kid, even if it means getting rid of all of you; so you'd better make sure this goes down smoothly, cause if we don't get rid of the girl at the concert, you're all history," he said coldly. "And, take care of this Angelina person and her husband. They need to have an unfortunate accident; a fatal one." Without further ado, he walked out the door.

"What are we going to do?" Mack exclaimed. "When I got into this, I didn't figure on killing anyone."

"What choice do we have?" Miss Nelson pointed out. "It's either them or us. Who is your best marksman?"

"Bob can outshoot the rest of us," the chief said, pointing to one of the officers.

"But to kill the little girl---she's only eight years old, same age as my daughter," the officer blurted out.

"Don't be so squeamish," Miss Nelson said. "Selling kids to be used for sex and pornography is not exactly a picnic for them: how could killing the little girl be worse than what we do?" She paused. "Bob, you're the shooter, so you can choose which one you shoot; Roseanna or her daughter; just be sure you get the job done. We'll meet again tomorrow night to go over plans for the rest of the operation."

Chief Bristol and Kent sat in the kitchen, at the ranch, going over the statement that Cassie had given. Mavis brought in a pot of fresh coffee, sandwiches and donuts.

"That should keep you awake for awhile," she said, leaning over and kissing Kent. "Goodnight, you two, I'm going to bed."

"Goodnight, honey," Kent said, returning her kiss. "It looks like it's going to be a long night."

The chief mumbled goodnight to Mavis as she walked out of the room. "There has got to be something in here that we are missing, some kind of clue, a common denominator that pulls all this together," he said, running his hand through his hair, despairingly.

"We've been over it time and time again," Kent said. "What could we possibly be missing?"

"Let's treat it as if it were a puzzle, with interlocking pieces, that are hard to find, but, that fit together perfectly when you do find them. You always have that first piece, the beginning, then you build around it."

Kent spoke up, getting into the spirit of the puzzle scenario. "The first part of this began the day that Cassie's mother was taken away."

"Let's look at the players in that part of the puzzle," the chief suggested. "There was Cassie's mother, the police officers, Miss Nelson the social worker, and of course, Cassie."

They went through the next part of the puzzle; the time Cassie spent on the streets, but came up empty-handed.

"There's no pattern here that I can see," Kent remarked.

The chief nodded. "It looks like this is a dead-end," he sighed. "Wait, a minute," he exclaimed, as his eye fell on a familiar name. He pointed to it. "This was the day Cassie was sold into the clutches of that man. See, whose name crops up on the very same day."

"Miss Nelson," Kent said, "but that really doesn't prove anything. She had a legitimate reason to be asking questions about Cassie, after all she was a run-away."

"Yeah, but remember she told Duke that she was trying to find Cassie to return her to her parents; she lied about that; and, later that morning was when Duke was approached by the man wanting to hire someone to do housework. That all fits together somehow, and, we're not leaving here until we figure it out."

"Let's go back to the day they took Cassie's mother to that mental hospital," Kent said, thoughtfully. "Why would they put her in there and put Cassie in a foster home, and, spend all that extra money, when, from what Cassie says, her mother was a stable person, and took very good care of her."

"Unless," the chief said slowly, as if figuring it out as he went along. "Unless, they never intended to put Cassie in a foster home, but was going to sell her into child slavery, and had to get the mother out of the way in order to do it."

"I believe the puzzle is coming together," Kent said, excitedly. "That day on the street, when Miss Nelson talked to Duke, she could have arranged for the man with the offer of work to be there, later, thinking that Duke would be the one to take him up on the job offer. He was just a street kid, and no one would miss him."

"No one would question it if Cassie and her mother suddenly disappeared either, they would probably just think

182

they had left to get away from her father's abuse; and the father sure wouldn't spend any time looking for them." The chief picked up the phone. "I want to find out if any other kids and parents in that area have come up missing under unusual circumstances."

"Do you think that offices in other cities that are supposed to help kids, could be in on this?" Kent asked. "This ring is widespread. I'm sure most of the folks who work in DHS and other programs for kids are honest and above board, giving of their time in order to help children, but, there could be a few scattered across the country that's in on this."

"We'll check it out," the chief said. "I've already got some people working around the country, but I'll put more people on the job. With this new lead concerning children's agencies, they'll have more to work with. We'll have to move quickly before the perverts running this slavery ring suspects that we are on to them; otherwise they will go into hiding and after some time passes, they will start all over again."

"We can't let that happen," Kent said. "We've got to bring these people down, now. The Bowman woman's disappearance will certainly trigger some kind of reaction from them. I just wish I knew how much they know, and what they are planning; I'm afraid it's going to spell trouble for Roseanna and her family."

"I think you're right," Chief Bristol replied. "I only hope and pray we can protect them."

"Amen to that," Kent said, a worried look on his face. He had put this family, whom he loved dearly, in danger; now he hoped he was able to protect them.

Chapter 22

Jesse sat at the desk in his office, wrapping up some last minute details, before leaving for the day. It had been a long day; it would be good to get home. The door opened and Pamela walked in.

"Do you have an appointment," Jesse asked, knowing that she didn't, and wondering if her unscheduled visit was meant to cause trouble for Belle and him.

"No, Jesse," she said. "I'm here to say goodbye."

"Goodbye?"

"Yes, I've taken a leave of absence from the firm, and I'm going abroad for awhile."

"Do you think that's wise, Pamela," he asked, concern in his voice. "It's only been a short time since you tried to kill yourself. I'm not sure you're ready to tackle the world just yet."

"I'm ready," she said. "Thanks to you, Jesse, I finally have my head on straight, and I don't want to sit around here and brood over the past. I want to face life head on, and live it to the fullest; and the best way to do that is to get far away from all the memories here. Don't worry about me."

"But I do worry about you," he said. "I'm partly to blame for the problems that caused you to take those sleeping pills, and I want to be sure that you won't try it again; so I wish you would have a few more counseling sessions with me, before you go traveling around the world."

"You worry too much," she said. "But I shouldn't be surprised; it was your caring ways that attracted me to you in the first place. I saw something in you that I had never

184

seen in another man.   I know you thought my kind of lifestyle was dirty and vile, and felt like you were the scum of the earth for being there with me; but by my standards, Jesse, you were a good and decent man. You were true to me even though you never loved me.   I knew you loved Belle; but you never let it show in front of me; at least not when you were sober. I saw the sadness in your eyes, and, I knew it was because you still loved her. I hoped as soon as the divorce was final, and we were married, that you would learn to love me, Jesse; but I always feared that the good in you would win out, and you would leave me one day." She reached over and touched his arm.   "A little of your goodness must have rubbed off on me because I'm here today, doing something totally out of character; something to help Belle and you."

She slipped the engagement ring, which he had given her, off her finger and handed it to him.   "I know you practically cleaned out your savings account to buy this ring; now, maybe you can sell it or hock it, and get part of your money back."

"I gave the ring to you, Pamela; you don't have to give it back," he said, offering it to her.   "It belongs to you..."

"No, Jesse," she said.   "I never had the right to wear it. The promises you made me the day you gave me the ring were not based on honesty or love; and, even though you tried to love me, your heart never belonged to me; your heart always belonged to Belle, and it always will."   A tear ran down her face.   "Jesse, I'm not good and decent like you. If I thought there was even a hint of a chance that I could get you back, I'd stay here and fight with everything inside of me; I'd take you away from Belle in a minute, if I thought I could; but I know that's a fight I could never win, so I'm throwing in the towel. I want you to be happy, Jesse, and I know you can only find happiness with Belle."

Tears misted his eyes. "Pamela, someday you will find the right man, and you will love him with all your heart…"

"I found that man, Jesse, but I found him too late; his heart belongs to someone else." She put her arms around him and kissed him. "Goodbye, Jesse. If you ever change your mind…" She turned and ran from the office, before she had second thoughts about giving up on this good man whom she loved with all her heart.

Jesse was shaken by her visit. He took a few minutes to compose himself, then, he picked up the phone and dialed Belle's number at work, hoping she was still in her office.

"Pecot Industries. This is Belle Lawrence, how may I help you?"

"Honey, you're never going to believe what just happened…"

"Angelina," Roseanna said, when her sister answered the phone. "Honey, I wanted to let you know how much we all want to be at your graduation…"

"I know, sis," Angelina interrupted. "I want all of you here so much, but I know you can't be; if those people in the slavery ring ever found out that you are my sister, we could be in a lot of danger."

"What's happening there? Have you had any flax concerning Rebecca's disappearance from the hospital?"

"Well, the hospital administrator and the police questioned me like they did everyone else, but I believe they were satisfied with my answers. I had an alibi for the time it happened. I was having lunch with Andy. Old Mr. Jones told his version of what he saw, and of course that cleared me of any guilt." She chuckled. "Someday, I'll tell you all about him, but right now I'll only say that he was one of the FBI agents working undercover there to protect me, and he did, when Dr. Blakely showed up unexpectedly, just as I was wheeling Rebecca out of the room."

"And, this Dr. Blakely, he didn't tell?"

186

"He couldn't," Angelina explained. "Chief Bristol and his men took him with them and they have him hid away somewhere. They made him call the hospital and say that his mother was very ill, so he was taking a few days off. I don't believe he's a part of all of this, but they couldn't take that chance."

"Will you be flying to Nashville for the concert?" Roseanna asked.

"No, we're driving through," Angelina said excitedly. "Andy bought me this great new sports car for graduation, a Jaguar XKR Silverstone Coupe, and I want to drive it home."

"Do you know how much that car cost?" Roseanna exclaimed. "Around a hundred thousand dollars."

"Andy spent that much on a car for me," Angelina gasped. "I had no idea. I'll be afraid to drive it now, for fear I'll get a scratch on it."

Roseanna laughed. "They drive like a dream," she said. "The prince had a Jag, and he let me drive it a few times. You're really going to enjoy it, but, please be careful, hon, and we'll see you in Nashville."

Roseanna had reserved an entire hotel in Nashville, close to the auditorium, for the ones who would be performing and working in the concert, as well as family and friends who would be attending, and, the agents who would be at the concert to make sure they were all safe. She, along with Brad and the kids, would be leaving for Nashville later today.

She was excited about the concert; it was the first time that Isabelle would perform before an audience, other than the congregation at church. Roseanna had written a special song for her, and Isabelle had been practicing day and night. She was determined to sing to perfection. She would need lots of practice with the band, in order that she could get used to singing with them, and they could learn

187

her method of singing, so they decided to leave a couple of days early.

Roseanna had chartered a jet to fly them to Nashville today, then, fly the rest of the family there the day of the concert, all except Steve and Jolee. They would be driving to the concert. She had just learned that she was pregnant; and, even though the doctor said it would be safe for her to fly; she didn't want to chance it.

Angelina sat proudly in the reserved section of the college auditorium along with the other graduates, waiting 'til her name was called and she could march across the stage and get her diploma. She was graduating with honors, the highest in her class. She glanced over to where Andy was sitting; he was looking in her direction. He smiled and waved his hand. She nodded, just as her row stood, and lined up. When her name was called, she marched across the stage, her shoulders back, her head held high. She had worked hard for this moment, and was proud of her achievements. She looked at Andy as she walked off the stage; he was grinning from ear to ear as he gave her the thumbs up sign.

They had packed all their belongings and shipped them home before leaving for the graduation service, so they left for Nashville as soon as the ceremonies ended.

"Do you want me to drive, sweetheart?" Andy asked as they walked to the car.

"No, I want to drive my gorgeous car, at least for a while," she said, sliding in under the wheel. "Thank you, honey, for giving me this wonderful graduation gift. I've never owned a car before, not even a ratty old jalopy."

Soon, they were out on the interstate on the first lap of their journey home. They would go by Nashville for the concert, and to see all the family and Cassie. Then they would go to Texas to visit Andy's family, then from there, home to the bayou. They had bought some property close to Brad and Roseanna, and after they had rested up for a few days, they would get started building their dream house. They chatted on and on about their future plans.

Andy kept glancing in the side mirror. A car, with one bright headlight and one dim headlight, had been behind them since they left the college. He hadn't thought anything about it at first, but now he was getting a little concerned. They had come several miles on this interstate, and he didn't like the odds that someone from the college would just happen to be going in the same direction they were, this far down the highway. There was only one way to know for sure if they were being followed.

"Honey, see that McDonalds ahead, would you pull in there," he said, casually, not wanting to alarm his wife. "I could use a bite to eat."

Angelina gave her signal to turn in. Andy watched the car behind them turn their signal on too.

"You must be starving," she said, as Andy grabbed her hand and almost ran into the restaurant.

She placed her order for a hamburger, fries, and a thick chocolate milkshake. "Honey, what do you want," she asked, nudging him in the side, as he stood gazing at the door, waiting for someone to come through.

"I'll take the same thing," he told the girl behind the counter, not taking his eyes off the door. His heart sank as a group of people came in at the same time. There was no way he could tell which of them, if any, was driving the car that was following them. Why hadn't he put Chief Bristol's private number in his pocket instead of packing it away in a box that was now on its way to the bayou?

"You seem a million miles away," Angelina said as they sat down to eat. "Is something bothering you?"

"I'm sorry, babe, I guess my mind was somewhere else, but, I promise to give you my undivided attention now."

"How about letting me drive that Jag," Andy said, nonchalantly, as they walked to the car. He didn't want to frighten her, but he knew they might have to do some fast driving if that car continued following them.

"Okay," she said, reluctantly handing him the keys.

Andy pulled out on the highway, keeping his eye on the road behind them. They traveled several miles down the interstate and he didn't see the lights of the other car. He was beginning to think that he had just been paranoid before, when, all at once, he saw it coming up close behind them; the car with one bright headlight and one dim headlight; and it was getting much too close for comfort.

This stretch of highway was deserted for miles. No houses, no lights, just forest and darkness. The only other sign of life was the headlights of another car, behind the one following them; too far away to help.

Andy pushed on the gas pedal. "I bet this baby can move," he said, hoping to get far enough ahead of the other car, that, he wouldn't have to tell Angelina what was going on. He pushed harder on the gas pedal.

"Andy, aren't you going a little fast?" she asked. "Please slow down."

"I can't, honey. There's a car that's been following us ever since we left the college and I've got to try to stay ahead of them, so hold on."

She looked in the side mirror. "Andy, they're getting closer! They're trying to go around us."

"Make sure your seat belt is fastened snugly, then, hang on. I think they're trying to force us off the road."

Andy raced down the highway at an incredible rate of speed. He remembered another time, another lonely road, and another sports car going at a high rate of speed. He remembered the crash; the horrible sound of steel hitting steel, and the two cars, lying mangled together in a twisted mass on the highway. He remembered sitting on the side of the road, holding Emily's lifeless body in his arms, rocking back and forth gently, as tears spilled down his cheeks and landed on her beautiful face. A face forever stilled; no more smiles, no more kisses, no more words of love, no more songs of joy, no more anything; his Emily was dead.

He pushed harder on the gas pedal, glancing now and then at the speedometer. He watched the numbers climb---100, 110, 115---he knew he was going too fast, but what choice did he have. The men in the car behind them were going to kill them.

"Andy! Angelina screamed. "That curve..."

He saw it too late to slow up and he was going much too fast to make it. He braked. He smelled the burning of rubber as the tires squealed, and the car skidded on the pavement as it was thrown into a violent spin.

"No!" he screamed. "Not again! Angelina!" He battled the steering wheel with all of his might, trying to bring the car under control, but he knew it was useless. "Angelina!" he screamed again; then silence.

Chapter 23

"Angelina," Andy called out, when the car came to a stop, just short of plunging into a deep ravine. He unfastened his seat belt and took his wife in his arms. "Angelina," he whispered, as she lay still. "God, no, please not again," he cried, then, let out a cry of relief as she stirred in his arms. "Angelina. Thank God!"

"Andy," she mumbled in a dazed voice, then screamed as it all came back to her, "Andy!"

"I'm here, baby," he said, holding on to her. "It's okay..." Just then he got a glimpse of the car that had tried to run them off the road. It was turning around. They were coming back to finish the job.

"Quick, honey, unfasten your seatbelt and let's get out of here," he said. "They're coming back!"

She tried to release her seatbelt, but it wouldn't budge. "I can't," she cried desperately. "It's stuck!"

He grabbed the fastener on her seatbelt and tugged with all his might, but it was no use.

"Andy, get out of here and make a run for it," she pleaded.

He shook his head. "I'm not going anywhere without you."

"Honey, please go. I don't want you to die, too."

He pulled her close. "I'm not leaving you. I'd rather die with you, than to live in this world without you," he said, kissing her. "I love you, sweetheart."

She clung to him, kissing him with all the love inside her as tears ran down her face. "I love you, too, Andy."

They sat there in each other's arms, preparing to die together. They braced themselves and clung to each other

192

as they heard squealing of tires on the pavement behind them. They waited for the bump that would send them careening off the road, to certain death in the ravine below. When it didn't come, they looked behind them. A different car was parked there. Several men were standing beside the car.

One of the men walked over. "Are you okay?" he asked, showing them his badge.

"FBI," Andy mumbled. "How did you get here so fast?"

"We were following, a safe distance behind you, and when we saw that you were in trouble, we speeded up immediately," he explained. "We had you in view all the time; Chief Bristol's orders. Unfortunately, the other car sped away when they saw us coming, and we didn't get a license number."

"Thank God; and thank you," Andy said with a sigh of relief. "My wife's seatbelt is stuck..."

"We'll take care of it," the agent said, and in a matter of minutes they pulled Angelina from the car.

After she calmed down a bit, Angelina looked the car over. "There's hardly a scratch on it," she exclaimed, happily. "Andy, my car is almost as good as new."

"Not for long," the agent told her. "We've got to push this car into the ravine..."

"Are you crazy," she gasped. "Do you know how much this car cost? Andy, please don't let them hurt my car."

"We don't have a choice," the agent said. "Officially, you both died in the crash, so we've got to make it look realistic." He motioned to a man dressed in a uniform and he joined them. "This is Sheriff Riley. We can trust him, but I'm not sure we can trust the local police. Since they were the ones that took Cassie's mother away, they may be a part of this. If they are, the men in the car that tried to run you off the road are working with them; so we've got to make this look convincing. We've got to make them believe that your car crashed…"

"What about the men in the car that was following us," Andy said. "They know we didn't crash."

"They will want to believe that you did, and will think that when you tried to back out on the highway, something went wrong and your car went over the embankment. They will not admit that they didn't do their job."

"That makes sense," Andy remarked.

"The sheriff will call the station and report the accident and they will come out to investigate," the agent continued. "They will find a burned car at the bottom of the ravine, and Riley will tell them there were no survivors. He will say that the bodies were burned beyond recognition, and have been sent to the crime lab for identification. But first, we've got to get you out of here, to a safe place." He nodded his head to the agent driving the FBI vehicle, and he eased up to the bumper of the Jaguar and gave it a little push.

Andy held on to Angelina, while she watched in horror, as her beautiful car went over the side of the embankment and exploded in a fiery crash in the ravine below.

"I'll buy you a new car, baby, as soon as we get home," he promised, trying to console her, but even the promise of a new car didn't make her feel better.

"I need to call Nashville and let our family know that we're okay," Andy said, when Angelina finally calmed down. He took his cell phone from his pocket.

"I can't let you do that," the man in charge said. "You're dead, remember? Not even your family can know about this."

"What if this gets out and they hear about our 'deaths'?"

"The lab won't identify your bodies for several days, and the police department here are certainly not going to let on that they know who was in the car, so there's no way your family can find out about this," the man in charge told them. "Now, let's get going, the sheriff has a phone call to make."

It was about an hour before the concert was to begin. Roseanna was sitting in her dressing room, alone, when a man walked in.

"How did you get in here?" she demanded, jumping up and moving away from him.

The man laughed boisterously. "It's me, Roseanna."

"Kent?" She shook her head, looking at the man standing before her. He had on a shoulder length wig, tied back in a ponytail; he also wore earrings, and glasses. "Why are you made up like that?"

"I'm one of your backup singers, remember, and I couldn't take the chance of being recognized."

"I don't think you have to worry about that," she said laughing. "I doubt if your kids would even know you in that get-up."

"Hon, I wanted to stop by and let you know that everything possible is being done to assure your safety…"

"I'm not so worried about myself," she put in. "It's Isabelle. I don't like the idea of her being up on stage in the limelight."

He frowned. "Roseanna, we're almost sure there is a shooter here tonight to try to stop Cassie, and we don't know what he may do in order to get to her. We've got several people in the stage area that will be monitoring everything closely," he said. "Besides me; there are the other backup singers, who are FBI agents; the keyboard man, and some of the backstage hands are also federal agents; put there to protect you and anyone else on stage, but, I can't absolutely promise you that we can keep you all safe, so if you want to call this off, there's still time."

I couldn't do that and live with myself," she told him. "If that bunch of lowlife scum got wind that something was up, they'd scatter, and you'd never catch them. That would mean that Cassie and her mother would be on the run for the rest of their lives; and those crooks would be free to prey on other innocent kids." Tears misted her eyes. "I'll admit I am scared, but I can't let it show. I've got to treat this like any other concert."

"Good girl," he said. "With all of us working together, we're going to catch those perverts tonight and put them away where they belong. I have a listening device in my ear," he said, pointing to the earrings, "so I'll know when all of them have been rounded up, and the coast is clear."

"Kent, do you know if Andy and Angelina are here yet," she asked, worried that they were running hours behind their scheduled time to arrive.

"I was just out there talking to your folks and they're not here yet. They were wondering if they might be back here with you."

"I haven't seen them and I'm worried; it's not like them to be this late and not call."

"They are probably so busy celebrating Angelina's graduation that they let the time slip away from them. Don't worry, I feel certain they'll show up any minute."

"I hope you're right," she said, still not convinced.

"I've got to get going, and make sure everything is in place, the way it is supposed to be," he said, kissing her on the cheek.

Belle and Jesse were sitting in the third row of the auditorium, beside Sara and her daughter. They had just met Brianna and were getting acquainted when all at once a hand tapped Sara on the shoulder.

"Do you mind if I sit here?"

Sara looked up. "Lance," she said, her eyes lighting up when she saw him standing there. She motioned for him

196

to sit down. "I'd like for you to meet my daughter, Brianna. Brie, this is Lance Pecot, a-a-friend of mine."

"I'm very pleased to meet you, sir," she said, extending her hand.

"I'm pleased to meet you too," he said, impressed by her good manners. "How did you get to be such a well-mannered young lady?"

"Mom and Dad taught me to always be respectful to my elders," she replied.

Jesse bit his lip to keep from chuckling out loud. Lance being called someone's elder tickled him way down inside.

Belle sucked in her breath. She had planned this reunion between Sara and Lance, hoping that once he met the little girl, things would work out for Sara and him. Now, for Brianna to call him old...

Sara quickly looked at Lance. How would he react to Brie's comment? She had hoped that their first meeting would be good, and, they would get along; she still loved Lance, and hoped someday to have a future with him; but would he ever warm up to her daughter now?

Jesse, Belle and Sara sat staring at him, waiting for his reaction.

"Your parents did a great job," he said. "It's a shame more kids are not taught to respect their elders." He took her hand. "I think you and me are going to get along very well. In fact, I would like to be your father, if you and your mother will have me."

"Lance," Sara scolded. "We talked about this."

"I know, honey, and I've given it lots of thought. I came to the conclusion that my life is not worth living without you, and, now that I've met Brianna, I know for certain that I want to be her father. Please, Sara, say you'll marry me."

"This is not the time or place..."

"Honey, it's exactly the right time and place." He leaned over and took her hand. "I love you, Sara; I want to marry you, and I'm not going to wait until this concert is over to get your answer."

"Lance, you know I love you…"

"Then why don't you marry him, Mama?" Brie asked bluntly. "I like him, and I need a new father to go along with my new mother."

Lance smiled. "That's two against one, so how about it. Will you marry me?"

"I see that I'm outnumbered so I don't have much of a choice," she teased. "I guess the only thing left to do is to set the date."

"We already have the license and the rings, so how about tomorrow while all our friends from back home are here," he suggested.

"What about your grandmother?" Sara asked.

"We'll phone her tonight and tell her the news. She can fly in on a private jet tomorrow in plenty of time for the wedding. She's going to be so happy."

"I guess it's settled then," Sara said. "There will be a wedding tomorrow." She turned to Belle. "Sam will be my maid-of-honor; her baby is due any day now, but, I think she can make it through the ceremony. I'd like for you to stand up with me too."

"It will be my pleasure," Belle said, all smiles.

Jesse was smiling too. This, all too handsome Romeo was finally tying the knot; tomorrow he would be a married man, and that made Jesse very happy.

"Jesse," Lance said, cutting into his thoughts. "I'll ask Ellis to be my best man, but I will need someone else to stand up with me, so will you do the honors?"

Jesse nodded, "I'll be glad to," he said, happy to be a part of something that would get his long time foe married, and divert his attention away from Belle.

The lights in the auditorium dimmed and the stage lights came on as the curtain slowly parted, and Travis Houston stood ready to get the concert underway.

"Folks, let's give a great big welcome to Nashville's own Roseanna!"

"Hello, Nashville." Roseanna greeted the audience in her usual manner, scurrying out on the stage. Then she burst into singing, "It's A Matter of Dreams"; still a favorite of her fans after all these years.

Cheers, whistles and applause almost brought the house down. No matter how long Roseanna stayed away, the fans still loved her.

"I'm going to sing a lot of your favorites tonight, along with a few new songs that I've written since the last time I was here," she said when the applause died down. She glanced at Kent, now and then, hoping he would give her the all clear sign. He shook his head slightly to let her know it was not over.

Bob, the shooter, was standing in the auditorium, waiting for his chance. He had gotten in without any problems by posing as a news photographer. His camera had a gun hidden inside, with a scope so he could zoom in on any target he chose. It also had a silencer so no one would know where the shot came from. Now, all he had to do was to focus in, and wait for the right moment. How long would he have to wait before the little girl sang?

Roseanna seemed calm on the outside as she performed to perfection, but her heart was pounding furiously, her hands were sweaty, and fear gnawed at her insides. She had put off bringing her family on stage, but she couldn't wait much longer. The concert would be over soon, and if she didn't introduce her family as she always did at every concert, it could raise suspicions. She glanced over at Kent. He shook his head slightly.

She turned to face the audience. "When I was here the last time, it was to say good-by. I was going home to have my baby, and I was planning to take time off to raise him. You know the story. We all thought my husband, Brad, and our daughter, Isabelle, had died in stormy waters off the coast of Florida. My world ended when I thought they were gone. I came to Nashville for solace and you gave it to me. I could not have made it through that horrible ordeal if not for all of you. But on Thanksgiving Day, that year, God performed the greatest miracle of my life; not only was my son born; but He sent Brad and Isabelle back to me. They had been stranded on an island in the Bahamas for eight months. God had picked them up out of those raging waters and put them down on the island, and now, I want you to meet my wonderful family," she said, motioning off stage.

Brad walked out on stage, holding the baby in one arm, and holding onto Will's hand with his other hand. Isabelle walked beside Jake, holding on to his hand.

"This dreamboat here is Brad, my husband and best friend, who just happens to be the most amazing man on earth." She leaned over and kissed him.

Applause rang out.

"That little guy who's checking out everything on the stage is Will; he's the baby I was expecting at the last concert; of course, he's not a baby anymore; he's big brother to the newest addition to our family, little Alex. We named him after our dear friend Maurice Alexander, who passed away a few months ago."

Brad held the baby up so the audience could get a good look at him; and, at Roseanna's prompting, Will stopped exploring long enough to wave at the crowd.

More applause followed.

"And, this beauty is our daughter, Isabelle."

The audience applauded as Isabelle smiled and threw kisses at them.

"This is Jake Andrews," Roseanna said, taking his arm. "Even though he's not blood kin, he is a member of our family. If not for him, only Will and I would be here tonight. He's the man who took care of Brad and Isabelle on the island; without him they would not have survived; he's the reason they came back home to me." Tears misted her eyes as a big round of applause went forth from the crowd, cheering this man who was responsible for putting happiness and joy back in Roseanna's life.

"The rest of my family is sitting out there; there's way too many to try to introduce, so let's give a big round of applause to all of them," she said, clapping her hands. "I'm so happy to have them here with me tonight."

Bob turned his camera toward the audience to try to find Roseanna's family; if he found them, he would find the girl. He had seen a picture of her and it was etched indelibly in his mind. He saw a couple of young ladies who looked enough like Roseanna, that, they had to be her sisters. He zoomed in and saw Cassie sitting with their group, surrounded on all sides by what must be FBI agents, guarding her. There was no way he could get to her unless he diverted their attention away from her. So he prepared to shoot Isabelle when she came up to sing.

Chapter 24

Roseanna had stalled as long as she could. As Brad and the others walked off stage, she took her daughter's hand. Applause rang out as they stood there, mother and daughter, looking lovely in the outfits that Mavis had designed. Roseanna was wearing an elegant close fitting, ankle length black gown, with sequins glistening across the bodice, and Isabelle wore a bright red gown with a full skirt, and a big bow in the back. "Father, watch over her," Roseanna prayed as troubling thoughts filled her mind. Was Kent right? Was there a shooter? If so, where was he, and, would he shoot an innocent little girl? "Folks, we've come to the part that you've all been waiting for," she said, as calmly as possible, knowing she had no choice but to let Isabelle sing. "I wrote this song a few weeks ago for my daughter to sing tonight, and, I know you're going to love the way she sings it."

The cheers grew louder as Isabelle walked to the center of the stage.

Bob focused in on the target and stood waiting for the right moment to pull the trigger.

"Thank you," Isabelle said, bowing and smiling that million-dollar smile that her mother was famous for. "The song I'm singing is called, "A Little Rock." I hope you like it." She nodded to the band and began singing in a voice that was akin to the voice of an angel.

"Hey, Little David, watching sheep, get a little rock,
Shepherd David, get your sling, get a little rock;
The hungry lion is coming your way,
He ain't had a meal all day;
Gonna face the lion, what can you say,

Get a little rock.

Hey, little David, watching sheep, get a little rock,
Shepherd David, get your sling, get a little rock;
The hungry bear is headed your way,
And he wants lamb chops for lunch today;
Don't give him a chance, stand in his way,
Get a little rock.

Hey, little David, watching sheep, get a little rock,
Shepherd David, get your sling, get five little rocks;
They've got our people scared to death,
Of all the Philistines, he's the best;
You're gonna face the giant in the final test,
Get a little rock.

Listen, Christian, it's your turn, get a little Rock,
Don't you know Jesus Christ, He's the Rock;
You're gonna face the lion, you'll meet the bear,
Turn around and the giant will be there;
Don't be helpless without a prayer,
Get a little Rock. Get a little Rock.
You're gonna face the lion, get a little Rock,
Gonna meet the giant, get a little Rock,
Gonna face the bear, get a little Rock;
Listen, Christian, it's your turn,
Get a hold of the Rock."

Isabelle curtsied and bowed as she finished the song. The crowd went wild as applause filled the auditorium.

"Mommy, they liked me!" she exclaimed as Roseanna rushed over and hugged her. "Do you want me to sing it again?"

Roseanna glanced at Kent. He shook his head. She knew the shooter was still out there, hidden somewhere in the audience. "No, baby, not this time. You were great, but I need you to hurry over to daddy, and stay with him."

Bob's hands were clammy; his brow beaded with sweat. He couldn't go through with it; he couldn't shoot the little girl. Every time he zoomed in, he didn't see Isabelle's face; he saw his daughter's face.

The photographer standing next to him turned and spoke to him. "Man, are you okay?" he asked, noticing the pale look on his face.

"Yeah, it's just a little hot in here," he said, cursing under his breath. He didn't want to draw attention to himself. Later, when this was all over, he didn't want anyone remembering him.

"I can shoot the woman," he told himself. "I have no qualms about shooting her. I am not a cold-blooded killer, but when it comes down to her life or mine..." He got Roseanna in his sights and waited for the perfect moment.

"Wasn't she terrific?" Roseanna bragged, clapping her hands and smiling proudly, as Isabelle walked off stage. She knew she would probably be the target of the shooter, but at least Isabelle was safe. "Thank You, God," she whispered, then bravely turned to face the audience.

"I'm going to sing one more song before the final song of the night. I didn't write this one, a man named Newton wrote it years ago, but it's still going strong today, and it's one of my favorites. I'm sure you know it, so sing along with me." She burst into singing stanzas of *Amazing Grace*.

Bob was sweating profusely now. Shooting someone down in cold blood was not easy, but he knew he had to do it. It was the only way he could get to Cassie; and if she walked out of here tonight, it meant certain death for him and the others.

Roseanna was mid-way through the song when he took careful aim; he would shoot her through the heart; that way it would be quick, and, hopefully painless. He steadied his hand, zoomed in precisely on the target and pulled the trigger. Then he turned pale as a ghost, and gasped in

204

horror. The instant he pulled the trigger, a bright yellow glow enveloped Roseanna, momentarily, then, seemingly, moved forward in his direction.

He cried out in fright and stumbled toward the door, mumbling incoherently.

The man who had spoken to him earlier, a federal agent, posing as a photographer, spoke into his radio. "Chief, there's a man leaving the auditorium, a so-called photographer. He's acting strange. He's coming out the main entrance, through the door on the left side."

"Yes, I see him," Chief Bristol answered. "We'll find out what's going on." He walked over to the man. "Sir, I'd like to ask you a few questions," he said, showing his badge.

"I did it. I shot her, just get me out of here," the man begged, "that thing is after me."

The chief looked at him, puzzled by his words. "Who did you shoot and what is after you?"

"The singer, Roseanna, I shot her right through the heart, but the instant I pulled the trigger this bright yellow glow was around her, and then it started coming at me. I've got to get out of here."

Chief Bristol opened the door to the auditorium and looked in. Everything seemed to be normal. Roseanna was singing as if nothing had happened.

"You say you shot Roseanna; but she's on the stage singing, alive and well."

"I'm an expert shot, one of the best, and I know my aim was true, but, that bright glow…it must have shielded her from the bullet, and now it's after me. Please get me out of here."

"Not until you answer some questions," the chief told him firmly. "What can you tell us about the child slavery ring?"

The man stood there silent.

"We know you're a part of it, so if you don't tell us what you know, you'll take the rap alone, and it won't go easy on you."

"They made me do this, so why should I let them go free while I rot in prison," the man said, looking around nervously. "I can give you names and addresses. I know the password to get into the computer where all the information is stored, and I also know where the hardcopy files are kept. The names of the customers and also the kids who were sold are all in there. I'll give you everything you need to bring them down, just get me out of here."

Kent," Chief Bristol said, "It's over, we've got the shooter, and he is talking big time, giving us the information we need to put that lowlife scum away forever."

"Thank God," Kent said, "I'll let Roseanna know."

Chief Bristol got on the phone to agents all across the country, waiting with the proper warrants to move at a moment's notice when the call came. They moved quickly, gathering the information out of the files in Miss Nelson's office; then they went to her home and took her into custody. Hoping to gain leniency for herself, she blew the whistle on the others. The agent's walked into police headquarters in Friends Harbor and arrested almost the entire force. The chief made a phone call to New York City and agents there took the big man of the operation into custody, amid cursing and threats, that they would lose their jobs for arresting him.

Roseanna finished singing "Amazing Grace" and glanced over at Kent. He smiled and nodded his head. "It's over," he said under his breath, mouthing the words so she could understand.

"Thank you, God." Roseanna breathed a prayer of gratitude. Her family was safe. Cassie was safe. They were all safe.

She turned to the audience. "My final song for the night is one that I wrote a month or so ago, and, I believe it was written especially for this concert. The song is entitled, "Red River," and, as I sing it, let the Spirit move in your life. God wants to do awesome things here tonight."

> *"You don't have to be too old to know about rivers,*
> *They bring life to everything you see;*
> *Waters come and rain, down the hillsides drain,*
> *Flowing through the valleys to the sea;*
> *There's a River that's overlooked by many,*
> *The very source of life my soul needs;*
> *The crimson stream of blood, Golgotha's cleansing flood,*
> *That old Red River that flows from Calvary.*
>
> *Red River from the Hill, flow to me and fill,*
> *The valley where I fall on bended knee;*
> *Send your rain from on high, don't let me run dry,*
> *Old Red River flow from Calvary.*
> *Old Red River flow from Calvary.*
>
> *This old River has been faced with opposition,*
> *The sands of time have tried to stop its flow;*
> *Down through the years it's still in good condition,*
> *It saved my life so many times I know;*
> *Every now and then I wander from the water,*
> *And that life stream can seem so far away;*
> *But, when I'm thirsty and dry, unto the Lord I cry,*
> *And, that old Red River starts to flow my way.*
>
> *Red River from the Hill, flow to me and fill,*
> *The valley where I fall on bended knee;*
> *Send your rain from on high, don't let me run dry.*
> *Old Red River flow from Calvary.*
> *Old Red River flow from Calvary.*
> *Old Red River flow from Calvary."*

Roseanna could feel the Spirit moving, so she nodded for Brad to come out on stage. He needed to take over now. God wanted to do something special in this place, and Brad would know what to do. She stepped back beside Kent and the other singers and they sang the song softly, over and over, as Brad stepped forward.

"Folks, the Spirit is mighty in this place," he said. God wants to do something awesome here tonight. Just open up your hearts and let Him do a work in you."

People all over the building fell to their knees in worship to the Lord.

Lance felt this weird feeling go over him. He didn't know what it was, but he knew he had to do something about it. He stood up and tapped Jesse on the shoulder. "Will you go pray with me?"

Jesse nodded, a bit surprised, but happy that Lance had finally decided to give his heart to the Lord. The two men made their way to the front and knelt down. Belle and Sara followed, tears flowing down their faces. They knelt beside the men and prayed for Lance to receive the Lord.

Lance stood to his feet a little later. "I never imagined it felt this great to be a Christian," he remarked with a big smile on his face and a glow about him that had never been there before. He grabbed Sara and held on to her as tears ran unashamedly down his face.

Belle put her arms around Jesse and drew him close so she could whisper in his ear. "Jesse, do you think we can go to Hawaii next week?"

He thought a moment. "Yeah, I think that can be arranged," he answered without grasping what she meant. Then it hit him. "Honey, does this mean…"

"Yes, God has worked a miracle in my heart tonight; all the hurt and resentment is gone, and I can't wait to go to Hawaii with my wonderful husband."

Brad had walked down from the stage and was praying with folks who had come up for prayer, when

208

suddenly a man ran to the front. He threw his arms around Brad and clung to him, tears flowing down his face.

"Preacher, will you pray for me?" he cried. "I need that cleansing river to flow through me, and I'm not fit to ask God myself, so will you ask Him for me?"

"I'll be happy to pray for you," Brad said, tenderly, "but you must also pray for yourself. God wants you to talk to Him."

"I can't," the man cried out. "God won't listen me, and I don't blame Him. I'm a vile hopeless sinner. I'm not worthy to go to God..."

"None of us are worthy of God's forgiveness, but He forgives us anyway," Brad explained. "Would you like to tell me what's bothering you? Sometimes it helps to talk about it."

He nodded. "Preacher," he said, tears running down his face. "I had a son, a wonderful little boy. He was everything a father could want in a son," He paused, momentarily, as the shame of what he had done engulfed him. "My wife had taken our little girl and left; my brother had moved in with my son and me. One day, Davy came to me, crying, telling me that his uncle had been molesting him ever since he moved in. I became angry that he would make up such a vicious lie so I beat him unmercifully, and told him never to lie like that again. Preacher, he didn't cry. He just stood there with a look of disbelief on his face. I wanted to pull him into my arms and beg him to forgive me, and tell him how much I loved him, but I didn't. That night he ran away and I haven't seen him since. I don't even know if he's dead or alive. I found out later that he was telling the truth." He fell to his knees. "Oh, God," he mourned, "Can You ever forgive me for hurting my son?"

Brad knelt down beside the man, praying with him, until he raised his head and tears of joy were rolling down his face.

209

Brad embraced him amid shouts of joy. Just then a hand tapped the man on the shoulder.

"Dave," a voice said, softly.

The man spun around. "Susan," he gasped, looking into the face of the wife who had left him all those years ago.

"Dave, this is all my fault, can you ever forgive me?"

"A few minutes ago, I would have spit in your face and told you to get lost, but God has forgiven me and made a new person out of me. He put love where hatred used to be, and He placed His Spirit within me, so yes, I will forgive you. And, this was not all your fault; if only I had listened when you tried to tell me about Cal, none of it would have happened." He took her in his arms, and they both wept, for the little boy they loved so much; the son they had so carelessly thrown away.

"Dave, is there enough compassion in your heart to take me back," she asked, tears brimming her eyes. "I want to come home; I've wanted to for years, but could never find the courage to try. Leaving you and Davy was the worst mistake of my life. Please tell me that you still love me and want me back, cause I've never stopped loving you."

Before he could answer a young girl walked up. Susan put her arms around her. "Krissy, here's your father…"

"Daddy," the young girl cried, running into his arms. She clung to him as tears ran down their faces. "Daddy, I've missed you. I want to come home."

"Krissy, I've missed you, too, and of course you can come home; both of you." He hugged and kissed her, his heart pounding with the joy of holding his daughter in his arms again.

"Daddy, have you found Davy? Do you know where my brother is?"

A sad look covered his face. "No, baby, I don't know where Davy is."

Cassie was standing close enough to hear part of the conversation. She walked over to the young girl. "Did your brother call you Honey?" she asked.

"Yes, how did you know?"

David and Susan Clayton grabbed hold of Cassie. "Do you know our son?"

"I think so," she told them, "but he doesn't call himself Davy, he calls himself Duke."

"Can you tell us where he is?" they asked eagerly.

"I don't know where he is right now, but I can tell you that he is safe, and that he is a wonderful boy; he took care of me when I ended up on the streets. I couldn't have made it without him."

Susan burst into tears. "He's been living on the streets...my poor baby."

"We'd like to hear anything you can tell us about him," Dave said.

"I'll be happy to tell you all I know."

Duke was sitting in the next to the last row in the middle section of the auditorium wishing he was anywhere else besides this place. It was too much like church, and, he had given up on church a long time ago.

The only reason he came tonight was because of Jake and Sam. They didn't want to miss the concert, and they had been good to him since he'd been hiding out at the mansion. Jake was the teacher at the home for girls, and after he had finished his regular day, he would spend hours catching Duke up on his education, from the fourth grade 'til now. Samantha made sure he had videos, movies, and all kinds of games to occupy his time. He was confined to his quarters, so no one would find out that he was there. He would do anything for them, even come to this concert.

He squirmed as this weird feeling came over him. "Okay, God," he said firmly, "Cut this out. I don't trust You anymore. You could have kept Uncle Cal from doing those things to me...You could have protected Little Flower from her old man...but You didn't. It seems like You're on the side of the bad guys and not on the side of kids like us, who need You. So, buzz off, I'm not taking the bait." He shuddered as goose bumps went up his spine, and he tried not to listen to the song that Roseanna was singing about the Red River of blood. He breathed a sigh of relief when the song was over. He looked around the room, trying to tune out the things that were going on up front.

His heart stopped beating as he saw a man walking across the back of the building coming right toward him. "Gus," he whispered, jumping over the seats and running toward the man. "Gus," he yelled, trying to be heard over the noise. He fell, weeping, on the man's neck. "Gus I'm sorry. Please forgive me. I didn't mean to leave you like that, but I was so scared. Gus, why did you give me your coat and blanket? Didn't you know you'd freeze to death in that alley without them? Why did you have to die?" He backed away as reality set in. "Gus, you're dead; and, I'm here with you, so I must be dead too. Did I die and not know it? Did God kill me for being disrespectful to Him?"

The man pulled Duke into his arms and embraced him. "Duke," he cried. "I've thought about you so many times." Tears welled up in the old man's eyes. "In the first place, boy, I am not dead and, there's nothing to forgive you for. You saved my life that day when you sent the policeman to check on me. He called 911 and they got to me in time to save my life. The nice officer went back to look for you, but you were gone. And, speaking of the nice officer, here he is," Gus said, as Kent walked up.

"How's it going, Gus," Kent asked, putting his hand on the old man's arm.

"You wouldn't believe me if I told you what just happened."

"After all that's taken place here tonight, I'd believe anything."

"You remember the young boy who sent you to check on me that morning when I was in the alley almost frozen to death; well, this is him."

"This is that boy?" Kent asked. "I went back looking for you…"

"I hopped a freight train that day and got as far away from here as I could."

"What are you doing back in Nashville, boy?" Gus asked. "You were always afraid your parents would find you, if you stayed here, since they live close by."

"The FBI brought me here. There was this outfit that sold kids into slavery and they were after me…"

"You're Duke!" Kent exclaimed. He knew the young boy was at the mansion, but he'd never seen him. "Come with me, there is someone who wants to see you."

"Little Flower!" Duke yelled, as he turned and saw her standing up front. He started running towards her.

"Duke," Cassie whispered, and ran to him. She threw her arms around him. "Duke, it's so good to see you," she cried. Tears were running down her face, as she embraced him. "Thank you for taking good care of me when I was there on the streets with you."

"But I sent you right into the clutches of that man…"

"Yeah, but because of the things you had taught me, I was able to get away from him, so you see, you were there for me when I needed you the most."

"Davy," a voice called out, and he turned to see who was calling him by his real name. She threw herself into his arms and wept. "Davy, I've missed you…"

"Honey?" he cried, stepping back to get a good look at her.

She nodded, and clung to him as he swept her into his arms and held her.

"You're all grown up," he said.

213

"I'm eleven," she told him.

"Do you remember me at all?" he asked, tears brimming his eyes as he held onto the little sister he loved so much, remembering all the good times they had shared, and angry about the years of her life that he had missed out on.

"Of course, I remember you," she assured him. "How could I forget? You were my big brother, my hero, and I loved you with all my heart. There's been an empty spot inside of me; and I cried myself to sleep every night for months, after mom took me away from you."

"Davy!" Susan Clayton called out as she turned and saw her son, standing there, so close to her. She ran and pulled him into her arms and kissed him hungrily, as six years of longing to hold him faded into the past. "Oh, son, I've missed you so much...please forgive me."

Just then the big strong arms of Dave Clayton, scooped them all up, and held them tightly. "Davy, I've found you, after all these years. Thank God you're okay. I love you so much, son, and, I'm sorry for what I did. Can you ever forgive me?"

Duke pushed them away roughly. "Forgive you," he sneered. "The two of you ruined my life; you took my childhood away from me. While other kids my age were sitting in a classroom, learning how to read and write, add and subtract, I was learning how to steal without getting caught. While they were out playing with their friends, I was trying to dodge street gangs, perverts, and cops. While they were in their beds at night, warm and safe, I was trying to find a box to sleep in, one big enough so it would shelter me from the freezing winter nights; and I was going through garbage bins in hopes of finding something I could use as a blanket, so I wouldn't freeze to death during the night." He shook his head. "Forgive you, I don't think so. And, don't thank God for taking care of me. He didn't help either."

His parents stood there speechless as he continued railing on them. "Mom, you left me behind for Uncle Cal to

214

molest...how could you do that. How could you not love me, I was your son..."

"Oh, baby, no," she cried. "I loved you with all my heart; leaving you behind was the hardest thing I ever did. But I was so scared for Krissy. I had seen Cal look at her in an evil way, and I was afraid of what he would do to her when he moved in with us. I never dreamed he would do that to you. I'm so sorry, and, I was coming back for you."

"And, Pop," he said, ignoring his mother's words, "you didn't believe me when I told you what that brother of yours was doing to me; instead you beat me with a belt; and, even though I didn't cry, every blow hurt worse than the one before it, and each time you hit me, I vowed that neither one of you would ever hurt me again. I ran away from you, and, I'm glad I did; living on the streets was much better than living with you."

His father pulled him into his arms. "Oh, son," he cried. "I am so sorry, and, I want you to know that every stripe I put on your back that day has been returned to me, fourfold, through the pain and guilt of knowing what I did to you, my little boy...you trusted me to protect you, but instead..." Tears rolled down his face. "I'm not fit to be your father, but, I do love you with all my heart. Please come back home so I can make it up to you."

Duke sneered mockingly. "Never," he said, with a cold hatred in his eyes. "I'm staying where I am. I like it there at the home and they are taking good care of me. Jake is teaching me, helping me catch up on the education that you took away from me; and his wife, Sam, is giving me the love that you didn't give me, Mom. She makes sure that I have good food to eat, a warm place to sleep, and provides all kinds of videos and games for me to enjoy." He paused a moment. "Gus also lives here in Nashville. He took me under his wing when I ran away, and ended up on the streets; he taught me how to survive out there. He's the only person who ever loved me enough to be willing to die for me." He paused again. "Go home with you, I don't think so; I'm staying here with people who love me; they're my family now." He turned and walked away.

Jake had been standing there long enough to hear what Duke told his parents. He held out his hand to Duke's father. I'm Jake Andrews," he said. "I'm so sorry about all of this."

The man grabbed his hand. "Thank you, for what you're doing for our son," he cried. "I don't blame him for the way he feels. He has every right to hate us. Do you think there's a chance he will ever change his mind and come home to us?"

"We'll do what we can to help him get over these feelings against you, but in the end, I believe only God can change his heart; and that may take a while," Jake said. "We're going to show him so much love that he will have to come around eventually. In the meantime, you're welcome to come visit as often as you like."

Cassie started after Duke but stopped suddenly when she saw Andy and Angelina walk in, along with a tall stranger, pushing a wheel chair. "Mama," she yelled, running to her. She threw herself across her mother's lap, laughing and crying with joy. "Mama, I was so scared when they took you away. I thought I'd never see you again."

Rebecca held her daughter close and stroked her hair. "My baby," she whispered, tears flowing unbridled, down her cheeks.

Andy and Angelina fell down beside Cassie.

"Thank you for finding mama and bringing her back to me," she said, hugging them.

The tall man standing there leaned over to Cassie. "I'm Doctor Blakely," he said. "I've been taking care of your mother and she is going to be all right. She'll need a lot of rest and tender loving care; but in time she will be as good as new."

216

"Rebecca," Franklin Cassidy cried, rushing over to his daughter, and pulling her into his arms. "My little girl," he whispered, as tears of joy made their way down his face.

"Daddy?" Her voice was weak but the smile on her face was radiant. As a child she had always felt safe when her father held her in his arms; now, his presence seemed to give her an inner peace that she hadn't felt in years.

"Mama, I found the wonderful little Baby you told me about, and, He's the One who helped me through all this, and brought you back to us." Cassie said. She stood and walked a few feet away from the others. She now understood about the free will that God had given to everybody and she realized that He had always loved her and watched over her "Thank You, God, for keeping Mama safe, for sending Grandfather Cassidy to us, and for Duke's family finding him after all these years." She felt a warm glow go through her as she stood in the presence of the Almighty Father; and she knew that He would always be with her and she would never again be a girl on the run.

Later, Cassie would tell her mother all that had happened in the months they were apart, but for now, just being together was enough.

Roseanna sat on the stage in the empty auditorium with her legs hanging over the side. Brad walked over and sat down beside her.

"Tired, sweetheart?" he asked, putting his arms around her and pulling her close.

She shook her head. "I'm just thinking of the things that happened here tonight," she replied, laying her head on his shoulder. "God is so awesome," she continued. "That man actually shot at me, and I would be dead right now had God not sent an angel to step in front of me and stop the bullet; and then the angel scared the shooter so badly that he confessed everything, and the FBI was able to round up all the perverts operating the slavery ring."

"And, they also got names of other children and the people who bought them," Brad said. "So, now those kids will be set free."

"Brad, I tremble when I think of all the awesome things that God did here tonight, as well the things He has done in all of our lives up until now." She paused. "It's like I can see this big tapestry; a tapestry of life where God is weaving the individual threads of each person's life. He patiently and lovingly weaves each strand in the way it should go. Take us for instance; the threads of our lives go along pretty steady for awhile, then, they are pulled apart, and it seems like the strands between us are broken, and can never be mended, but God takes each thread and tenderly weaves it in a direction that brings us back together." She wiped away tears that were blinding her. "And, Belle and Jesse; we had all given up on them. It seemed as if the devil had frayed the fabric of their lives beyond repair, but God took that same fabric, mended it, and made it good as new. Belle told me that they are going to Hawaii next week, that God performed a miracle in her heart tonight, and all the hostile feelings against Jesse are gone."

"Thank God," Brad said, breathing a sigh of relief. "And, what about Lance giving his heart to the Lord; you've got to admit that was indeed a big miracle."

"Yes," she said. "Belle and I have prayed for Lance since we were kids, and I was about ready to give up on him. I'm glad God never gave up on him."

"God is so good," Brad remarked reverently. "I'm still in awe of all the miracles that took place here tonight."

She nodded. "I think maybe the biggest miracle was what He performed in Cassie's life," she said thoughtfully. "Do you realize how long God had to work on the threads of so many different people's lives in order to make everything work out for her, and, how He brought it all together tonight?" She paused a moment. "He started weaving the threads years ago, that would put Andy at the right place, at

218

the right time, in order to save Cassie from that man. When God sent him into my life, I thought it was just to help me through the bad times, when I thought you and Isabelle had died; but now I realize there was a dual reason for Andy coming into my life, 'cause otherwise, he would never have met Angelina, fallen in love with her, married her, moved to Friend's Harbor, and ended up on exactly the right street to rescue Cassie."

"And, God had worked on Angelina years before to cause her to choose that college," Brad pointed out. "That also put her at the right place to find Cassie's mother and get her out of that hospital."

"And, there's Duke," Roseanna continued, "Cassie could never have made it on the streets without him, so God worked it out that he would be on the exact street where she would end up when she ran away. It's a long way from Nashville to Friend's Harbor, and Duke could have gone anywhere, but he ended up there."

"And, God brought all of them here tonight," Brad said. "What a great miracle for Dave and Susan Clayton to find their son after all these years; and to know that he is alive."

"Do you think Duke will ever forgive his parents and go back home?"

"I don't know," Brad said, shaking his head sadly. "The hurt they have caused him is so deeply imbedded inside him, that right now, he doesn't want to forgive them. I'm not sure he ever will, unless he turns it over to God; for only God can heal the hurting in his heart. And, he's not ready to turn to God for help yet. We can only pray that someday he will be."

Tears misted her eyes. "Brad, I'm so thankful to God for weaving our lives together in such a beautiful pattern. I think of all the uneven stitches and broken threads, caused mostly by me, when I chose to detour from the way He had planned for me; and I marvel at how He patiently mended the broken stitches and straightened the uneven ones to get me back on track, so the threads of our lives could run in a smooth pattern again." Tears were running down her cheeks now. "Honey, I'm thankful, too, that God chose you to be my husband, my partner in life, for truly, I don't believe I could have made it this far without you by my side. And thank God, He gave you grace enough to put up with me and to love me all these years. There were times that I certainly didn't deserve your love."

He pulled her close. "Sweetheart, I'm thankful God put us together, too, for I would not want to walk through life without you, either."

"God has woven the fabric of our lives into such a beautiful tapestry," she remarked. "We have each other, three great kids, a loving family, lots of good friends, and a wonderful home in which to enjoy all the good things He has given us. Our world is so perfect."

A slight frown crossed his face, as he jumped off the stage and lifted her down. "Sweetheart, what if God should want us to walk down a different road, an unfamiliar one; one that would take us far away from home and family?"

"Then, my darling husband, we will walk, hand in hand, down that road together."

He kissed her and silently thanked God for this amazing woman standing here beside him.

"God's great tapestry of life," she mused. "Maybe I'll write a song about that." She grabbed Brad's hand and they walked out the door, letting it swing shut behind them.